The Subtle Truth

Robbie Brown

Subtle Truth
by Robbie Brown

Copyright © 2022 Robyn Lynn Stokes
All rights reserved
ISBN: 979-8-9867703-07

A
Speak Life Publishing
Novel

Dedications

This book is dedicated to my hero and my daddy, Robert Brown. It's also dedicated to my shero and auntie, Seedso. (Marilyn Cole-Arrington)

May they rest in peace.

Lastly, my children: PJ, Brittany, Nicole, and my grand-daughter Milani you all are my life.

Acknowledgements

Thank you to the love of my life, Amound. You believed in me day one. When we came together, you immediately said that you wanted to help me complete this book. Thank you for being my biggest cheerleader.

Dr. Angie, my Sisco (cousin/sister), I can't thank you enough for taking this journey with me. You made me realize that I am an 'A' student and capable of writing another book. You have no idea how much your help meant to me. I appreciate you and all that you have done for me.

Kiri, my other sisco, thank you for beleiving in me and assisting me through this journey too. You have been a rock during this writing period.

Mom thank you for always being there and believing in me. I truly appreciate your words of encouragement throughout the entire process.

Adrienne, thank you for reading all the different versions of my manuscript. You have been a valuable source of positive inspiration.

Chapter One

Rising from the floor while holding my throbbing face, I had just received a fierce backhand knuckle slap from Malik. With blurred vision from watery eyes, I can barely see my surroundings. Where am I? What happened? Oh yeah, I remember as my vision comes into focus. I look at him in disbelief. He did it again!

Malik promised to never put his hands on me after the last incident a few months ago. We were fresh into our romance. He got mad because I sat at the lunch tables with Jeremy after my math class. We were going over some math problems Jeremy didn't understand. Malik walked up to the table with his boys. He glared at Jeremy with a flared nose, arched brow and wrinkled forehead that indicated he was angry. His face was tense and stiff. Malik's face always did that when he was mad.

"Jazz! Whatchu doin with this foo?"

Still glaring at Jeremy with raised shoulders and a balled-up fist, antagonistically waiting for a response. That was the first time I encountered him talking like that. He was clearly jealous. I had never seen him like that before. Maybe it was because I was always with Mimi and never with a boy.

"Malik why you talkin' like that?
Jeremy needed help with a math
problem we had in our last class."

Malik sucked his teeth, sighed, turned around and walked
away while shaking his head. His boys followed his lead.
Jeremy was so engrossed in completing the problem he didn't
realize Malik was mad about him being with me.

"Hey Jazmyn, is that your boyfriend?"

"Yeah, it is."

"He needs a hood rat. You are too
pretty for him."

"Wow! Thanks Jeremy. That's very
sweet of you to say, but Malik and
I are fine."

After school that day, I went to Malik's house. Upon entering
the room, he grabbed me by my arm and threw me on the
bed. "Malik what's wrong with you?" I yelled. He climbed on
top of me and gripped his hands around my throat. He spoke
through his teeth, "Don't ever let me see you sittin' with
another dude at school." As Malik grew in anger, his hands
gripped tighter. I was gasping for air. He noticed my eyes
starting to roll to the back of my head. This is the first time he
placed his hands on me. My mom once told me, "When a dog
tastes blood, they will always want more and more. So, you
must put that dog to sleep before it bites you again." Now, I
understand what she meant. At any rate, this dog had his hands
around my neck. I had to think fast. I played dead. I went
limp. Maybe he will feel sorry for me. He may have a
remorseful bone in his body and stop. It worked.

"Jazzy! Baby! Wake up! Wake up!
I'm sorry, please wake up!"

He was afraid he had killed me. I took three long desperate
gasps for air and I blinked a lot. While looking at him I
exhaustingly answered, "Yes."

"Baby, baby, I'm so sorry I won't put
my hands on you again. I promise. I
promise. I love you so much. You're
my everything."

Yes! I got him. My best Academy Award winning
performance; and yet, he did it again!

This time it was a backhand knuckle slap. That slap was
serious. For a second, I couldn't breathe. I'm so scared. He
won't look at me or even talk to me. I cry silently. All of this
catches me off guard. I have no idea what to do. I escape to the
bathroom, but don't want his grandmother to see me crying.
So, I walk as quietly as I can into the bathroom. I look at my
arm. I must make sure I don't see any bruises. Malik gripped
my arm so hard it left a purple handprint. It hurts so bad. Why
did he get so mad? I'm confused. I return to the room.

"Malik, why did you do that?"

"Don't ask stupid questions!
Why you lookin' at my phone?"

"You think I'm cheetin?"

"Noooo, I was just looking for
a picture of us. I wasn't trying
to be nosey. I promise."

"Get outta ma house!"

I grab my backpack and leave his house in haste. My face is still throbbing as I closed the door. It hurts like crazy.
An incessant pounding in my jaw like someone is beating on a kettle drum. It feels almost like he disconnected one side of my face from the other side. I'm certain something is loose in my head. That boy has some serious issues! I never thought that he was abusive when I met him at Spring Canyon High School. He was a junior in my freshman year. I thought he was so cute with his fresh low haircut, long eyelashes, light mustache, and dark brown eyes. He is 5'10" and skinny. He dressed like a neat thug. His pants sagged a little, not quite to his butt, just enough to indicate that he was at least a part time thug. He did wear a belt to make sure his pants didn't fall off. His tennis shoes looked brand new all the time. I loved him then, but I'm even more in love with him now. Oh look, there's a McDonald's. I think I'll stop in there to check my face for marks before I go home. Uncle B and Auntie Rachel might notice. They never miss much with me. Wow! This place is always crowded.

"Excuse me, pardon me, excuse me.
I just want to get over there. Thanks."

I hope that I don't see anyone I know in here. Let me go to the restroom. Good, it's empty. I will just lean over the sink to examine my face more closely. Look at me! I can barely touch my face. One cheek is swollen and red. My eyes are bloodshot from tears. I need some make-up to cover these very noticeable bruises. I'll take my hair down so that it will cover the sides of my face. That way, no one will see anything. Ugh! My eyes! If only I had a pair of shades, I could hide my crying puffy red eyes. Look at me! What is wrong with that boy! I'm a mess! Okay, I gotta get out of here.

I'll just order some fries and go home. I hope I don't get that one boy to take my order. He always messes it up. Ooo! This will work, no line. Ohhhh no. I can't believe it. A shift change and it's that boy from "Stupidsville." Ugh! Not again. Okay, calm down. I'm just getting fries. There's no way he can mess that up. He calls me up.

"Next!" I clear my throat.

"All I want is a LARGE,
HOT order of friiiieeeesss."

I explain slowly and clearly.

"Okay you just want a large
order of fries."

"No! A LARGE HOT order
of fries. Did you hear the hot part?"

"Yeah, that will be $5.02."

"Wait, $5.02? Serious? They
were $2.75 last week."

"Did you come on a Wednesday?"

"Yeah, I think so. What does
that have to do with the price?"

"They are $2.75 on Wednesdays.
Today that will be $5.02."

I paused. I'm hot. This guy thinks I'm stupid.

"Here, take the money and make
sure they are HOT!"

I stand to the side and wait. If he messes up my order, I'm
going to do to him what I should have done to Malik. I hear
my number. I get my bag and check it. Inside the bag is a
happy meal for kids! There is a toy, chicken nuggets, small
cold fries and a milk. Ugh! Forget it! I'll eat it. I just need
to get home. See! See! Malik brought all of this on me. If he
had kept his hands to himself, I would not be having all of
these problems. What's wrong with that boy? He was the
coolest guy in school. The cutest guy by far, before he dropped
out. Malik has so much freedom and that fascinates me. He
doesn't have a curfew and never tells anyone where he is
going because he lives with Big Mama.

Big Mama is Malik's grandma. She's a five-foot ten inch,
220lbs, beautiful black woman from Alabama. Her voice
always rings through the house when she speaks. I noticed her
hands have scars on them. She told me it's from working in
the kitchen at a restaurant for over twenty-five years.
Big Mama's skin is perfect. She has no wrinkles, a head full
of long, wavy, silky black hair. In fact, when she combs it
forward, it falls past her knees.

Big Mama is a housedress wearing woman who loves to watch
all of the court shows that come on TV. She always has a
whole bunch of kids around the house. Too many kids to
worry about Malik. As far as she is concerned, he can take
care of himself. Malik told me that Big Mama came into his
life when his mother left the family: Malik's dad, Omar and
himself. His parents were teenagers, who had no clue how to
care for one child let alone two.

She helped Malik's dad, Bobby, while he finished high school. When he was accepted into college, Big Mama encouraged him to go. She didn't know he wouldn't come back. This is really a sad story. I really feel for Malik. Many people have sad stories like his, but it's not an excuse to abuse me. Enough of Malik for now, I need to figure out how to get in the house incognito.

Chapter Two

Rrrrringg! Jumping from my desk with my backpack across my shoulders, I dashed down the hall like a sprinter coming out of the starting blocks. Gracefully, I dodge the crowd to seek my bestie at her locker. Mimi Springer, a 5'7", average looking girl with Hershey chocolate brown skin and long black braids flowing to her butt. She talks very loudly like the braces on her teeth are too tight and giving her a bad connection with the cell towers. Maybe those big hoop earrings she wears have something to do with how loud she speaks. Nevertheless, Mimi is a very sweet person who knows all my secrets. I can trust her with my life, but I can't tell her about what Malik does to me.

"Hey girl, why are you in such a hurry?"

"I'll tell you as soon as we get off campus. I can't say now. There are too many nosey people at school that are waiting to tell your business as soon as they hear it."

"Okay, but I need to find Danny to tell him bye, and to get my house keys from him."

Mimi says as she looks around for Danny.

> "Mimi! Why does he have your
> house keys?"

> "It's a backpack thing." She answers.

> "Whatever. Man! Mimi COME ON!
> We have to go! Doesn't he go to
> his locker when he gets out of class?
> Go to his locker first. You might
> catch him there; and come on!"

> "If he doesn't have football
> practice, he'll go."

She stands on her tiptoes to see over a sea of kids.

> "I'll meet you at the gate.
> Give me like five minutes.
> I'll be fast."

Mimi drops her backpack at my feet and takes off running.
She didn't want me behind her yelling to hurry up, nor did
she want me to leave her. As I get to the gate to wait for
Mimi, I see Malik sitting in a car waving me over. The
music is loud, all the windows are down, and the bass is
pulsating. I look over and see L.T. in the driver's seat. He
is one of Malik's stupid friends.

I roll my eyes and walk over. I'm not in the mood for him right now. Malik knows I can't stand that ole stupid boy.

"Hey sexy, you coming over today?"

Malik speaks with his eyelids low. I'm immediately irritated because he is in the car with L.T. and high.

"Naaaaahhhh, I'm gonna go to Mimi's."

I answer looking past the hood of the car.

"Wassup Witchu? Why you got an attitude?"

He says as he licks his lips. You know how LL Cool J licks his lips. I love it.

"Malik, why are you up here?"

"I'm up here with my homeboy. Man, I'll check you out later."

He turns to his boy. "Let's roll man." L.T. is talking to a girl. He's trying to get a date, a kiss, her number or something. Whatever it is, she is not feelin' it. Maybe, if he turns the engine off he would get some action. That loud rumbling sound, from his Camaro engine, is too much of a distraction for her. All she is saying is, "Huh! What! Huh!" Huh! It's kind of funny though. L.T. gets mad and speeds off. Mimi walks up.

"Was that...Malik?"

She says pointing her finger in their direction..

"Yeah, it was him." I mumble.

"What is he doing here?"

"I don't know. He said that he
was hanging with his homeboy.
I don't care right now. We have
to get to the store. I need a
pregnancy test."

Mimi grabs my arm and pulls me back in mid-stride. We
stop. Mimi places her hands on her hips. She leans to one
side so the backpack won't fall off her shoulder.

"We have to get a WHAT?"

"You heard me!"

We start walking again.

"Jazz, are you serious? You're pregnant?"

Mimi screams.

"Jazmyn you are so pretty and
petite. You know what happens
when you get pregnant? Your
100lbs, 5'2" frame will be jacked
up. Your smooth caramel skin
will be all bumpy, and your
complexion may get a few shades
darker. Well, that's what happened
to my sister.

All of that naturally curly long hair
will probably get longer since
you're pregnant, which is good.
You might like that. All the crop
tops you like to wear will be mine.
Stretch marks will destroy that
beautiful flat stomach and make it
look like a road map. I will also take
all of your Jordans because your feet
will swell and you won't be able to
walk or put them on. In fact, my
mama said after she had me, her feet
didn't return to the normal size. Oh
yeah, your daily bag of hot Cheetos,
you just love so much, will probably
make you sick. For nine months you
will be uncomfortable with only a
bad attitude to show for it. Now I see
why you frown so much. It's because
you're pregnant! I really miss your
beautiful smile with those perfect
teeth. Jazz, I've always loved your
smile and I don't see it anymore.
The way you've been acting lately
makes sense now. You're pregnant."

"Stop saying I'm pregnant over and
over. I'm getting the test to see. That's
what they are for, right? To see if I'm
pregnant."

"Whatever. Let's go get the test"

Once in the store, I have no idea what to look for. There are so many Home Pregnancy Tests to choose from. I need the one with the fastest results.

"Mimi, which one should I get?"

I ask while looking on the shelf. She looks at me like a deer in headlights.

"How am I supposed to know?"

Mimi replies while handing me a pink and white box. "Quick Answers Pregnancy Test." I read out loud like a fool so all can hear.

"Shhhh…why are you so loud? You want everybody to know you might be pregnant?"

"Oh, was I loud?"

I pick up another box and begin to walk toward the register. I'm afraid. It's like walking the longest mile. I can hear my momma saying, "Jazmyn honey, you have to walk with purpose so people will take you seriously when you enter in a room. You can't walk with your shoulders slumped over and your head down. Stand up, back straight and hold your head high with exuberant confidence." I never thought I would have to find confidence to walk to the register at CVS. I also never thought that I would be paying for a pregnancy test either. My feet feel heavy. It feels like I'm walking in slow motion. This register is so far away. Is someone pulling it further away from me? I hide two boxes under my hoodie until I got to the register. Mimi stands at the door. I'm not sure if she was embarrassed or sees something interesting.

I place the two boxes on the counter. The cashier looks at
the test. Then, looks at me over her reading glasses.
That'll be twenty forty-five." I slam my money on the
counter, grab the tests, shove them in my backpack, and
impatiently wait for my change. The cashier slams the change
back to me on the counter. I snatch it up and walk away. I
didn't want to be rude, but that made me mad. She's so rude.
Once outside Mimi and I run to her house at the speed of light.
We normally stop at the liquor store, but not this time. We fly
pass that neighbor who likes to water her grass when we walk
by. She always has water all over the place. We run by her
so fast it was like we were sailing on the water. Mimi gently
touches my arm, and we stop running. I'm glad because I had
to catch my breath.

> "Jay, I think I saw Destiny Monroe
> in the store while you were paying."

> "Yes, that was her. I noticed her
> looking between the aisles."

> "I hope she didn't hear anything.
> If she did, the whole school
> will know something in twenty
> minutes."

We start back to the house and arrive in record time. She opens
the door and I push pass her to the bathroom. I begin to pull
the boxes out of my bag. I can feel my heart racing. My hands
are shaky. I can feel sweat forming on the back of my neck
where the hood of my jacket is. I rip the box open and pull the
stick out. I am really taking a pregnancy test. Me, pregnant.
I stop for a second to skim the directions. It says to hold the
stick in the stream of urine. That sounds really gross, but this
is what I have to do.

I wonder if I should get some gloves, to hold the stick, so I won't pee on my hands. "Well, Jazz, I guess we are about to do this." I say to myself. I look in the mirror and don't recognize my face. It looks a little chunky. I lean closer to the mirror over the sink to take another look. My eyes look sad. The shock of being pregnant is devastating. I take a step back, pull my pants down and squat over the toilet as I hold the stick in place. The moment of truth is here. I'll understand why I hate the smell of Auntie Rachel's food, and why I can't stay awake for more than five minutes. If the test is negative, then something could really be wrong with me. I don't want to look at the test, but I have to. I look at it. The words say pregnant in bright pink. I throw it on the floor, pull the other box out, rip it open, and try to pee on that stick. There's nothing left. I can't go.

Leaning on the bathroom wall with my pants still down, I sob. I'm only fifteen years old. What am I supposed to do? How do I tell Malik? How am I going to take care of a baby? Where is my mommy when I need her? So much to think about. I don't know anything about taking care of a baby. I have never even babysat. I was so stupid to let Malik convince me to have sex with him. He even convinced me to have it unprotected. I never even gave pregnancy one thought. We had sex many times and not once did I think there was a chance I could get pregnant. What was I thinking? This is bad. It's all bad. Mimi knocks on the bathroom door.

"Jay, you okay in there?"

I didn't answer. I rise to pull my pants up and wash my face. I look at my eyes again in the mirror.

"Jayyyyy, you okay? Talk to me."

I can tell Mimi is talking through the cracks around the door. She sounds so serious.

"I'm good."

I quickly grab a towel and shove my face in it.

"Aaaaaahhhhh!!!"

I scream and lament.

"I'm coming in there."

Mimi uses the key they keep above the door to come in. Once she's inside, I can't control my tears. Mimi walks over and hugs me from behind. She gradually stands me upright. She knows the results. I point to the test on the floor.

"It's gonna be ok, Jay. I'm here
for you."

When I finally stop crying, I sit on the covered toilet seat. Mimi sits on the cold bathroom floor staring at me.

"Jaaaayyyy, you pregnant.
What are you going to do?"

"Mimi, stop. I don't need
anyone to be my mother
right now."

"I'm not tryin' to be yo mama girl,
I'm tryin' to be your friend and see if
you know what you're gonna do."

She picks the test stick up with a tissue and hands it to me. I grab it, put it in the box and place it in
my backpack.

Mimi asks, "Well, what are you
going to do?"

"I don't know. I'm not gettin' any
abortion though, know that."

"You're fifteen! You can't raise a baby.
Are you stupid?"

"I can't kill a baby either. Malik and
I can do this together."

There's a lot to think about and I'm only fifteen years old. I
remember my mama telling me, "When you grow up too fast,
and do adult acts, you will suffer adult consequences. You will
be forced to make adult decisions." It's really tough to do that
when you are not an adult. I begin to straighten my clothes and
smooth my hair. My eyes are super puffy and bloodshot red.
It feels like the room is closing in. I'm suffocating because
of the pregnancy test. I need to escape. I run out of her house
and do not stop until I reach my front door. All of a sudden,
my feet feel so heavy. It's like I'm wearing brick tennis shoes.
"Oooooohhhh noooo, I'm pregnant." My hands are shaking as
I try to put the key in the door. I can't focus with blurry vision
from runny puffy eyes. It took me a few minutes to finally
stick the key in the door. "Auntie Rachel! Uncle Benny! You
home? Is anyone here?" I yell upon entry. No answer. Perfect!
No one is home. I walk straight to my room, get the test out,
and slam my door shut. Wow! I'm pregnant. Tears form in my
eyes thinking about the negative reaction Malik might have to
my pregnancy. We never talked about me getting pregnant.
We never thought it would happen. Although I was young
when my mom died, we always had long conversations.

When she got pregnant with my sister, she explained a lot
about pregnancy to me. Now that I'm in this position, I
understand what she was saying. Mommy emphasized
that I should be married when I get pregnant. She also
told me the cost to have a child is expensive and
someone must have a job. Her pregnancy was easy, but
she told me there could be complications with the
pregnancy and during childbirth. I was shocked
that there could be something wrong at any time.
The baby could be still-born. It could even die minutes
after birth. Also, it could be born with special needs.
Some of the conversations I had with my mom seem
to be ahead of my time. Maybe God told her to tell me
those things because He knew she wasn't going to
be here when it happen to me. After all, God does
know everything. Now, I understand why I should be
older and married. It takes two to raise a baby just like
it took two to conceive it. Sadly, I have to deal with
Malik and his temper. His temper scares me. I
shouldn't feel this way with someone who says they
love me. I shouldn't allow him to do those things to me
either. When he gets physical with me, I have no idea
what to do. My phone chimes. It's Malik.

> *Malik - Hey, Bae you still at Mimi's*
> *doing homework?*
> *Jazzy - Yeah*
> *Malik - I miss you. Will I see you tomorrow?*
> *Jazzy - Probably*
> *Malik - You know I be missin you when*
> *you don't come over. I can't stand*
> *when I don't see your beautiful*
> *face every day.*
> *Jazzy - I'll probably see you tomorrow.*
> *I have to hit you later, ok?*

Malik -Hey, wait, why are you rushing me
off? You can't text me now like you
always do? I don't wanna hear that
messs about school either.

Jazzy - I have to go.

I hate it when he talks to me like that. I'll just turn this phone off and put it in my backpack, so I won't be tempted to talk to him. "Mommy, I need you. Why did you guys have to leave me here by myself?" I whisper while looking at the ceiling. For some reason, I wait expecting an answer. I really miss their input. The pain from their absence is magnified by these situations. I feel so alone and lost. I need their help. I'm sure they would be upset with me, but they would still love me and be here for me too. When I was ten years old, we were in a bad car accident. A drunk driver ran a red light and hit our car, killing my mom and dad instantly. Uncle Benny, my daddy's brother, and Auntie Rachel, his wife, came and picked me up from the hospital when I was well enough to leave. They took me in and I have been living with them ever since. My only problem is Auntie Rachel. She doesn't want me here and does everything in her power to irritate me. She's a short fat, hobo slob of a woman. She is always wearing ugly wigs even though her hair is pretty without them. She also wears glasses that cling to the end of her nose. Her dark brown skin is so smooth and pretty. I always thought she was beautiful, just mean.

"Jazmyn…Jazmyn?"

Auntie Rachel knocks on my door. "Yes!"

I hadn't realized I'd fallen asleep. It happens a lot. I'm always tired.

"You okay, honey?"

"Yeah, just tired."

"Well Uncle Benny bought dinner,
so wash up and come eat."

I hope he got something good to eat. I'm starving. Auntie Rachel must be in a good mood. She's actually nice to me. I walk into the kitchen.

"Hey Punkin, I bought your
favorite food, Panda Express."

He exclaims smiling from ear to ear. He is the best. She, on the other hand, ugh, I can do without. Uncle Benny is my favorite Uncle in the whole world. He is fun. He likes to talk to me. He also likes to listens to what I have to say. No one really wants to hear what I have to say, at least not adults. Uncle Benny often tell stories about when he and my dad were growing up. He has a million great pictures of them that he shows me. Uncle Benny makes me feel very close to my daddy. I feel like I'm connected to him. They didn't look-a-like, but anyone could tell they were brothers. Uncle Benny isn't very tall, but he is a jolly man. He's a lighter version of my daddy. Uncle Benny has aged over the years I have lived with him. His caramel bald head was once covered with tons of hair. His beard is now gray, but he keeps it nicely trimmed. Uncle Benny is always neatly dressed. I have never seen him wear anything baggy, dirty, or raggedy. My Uncle Benny is a very well kept and handsome man.

> "Look, I got all your favorite choices.
> There's noodles, steamed veggies,
> black pepper chicken, and orange chicken."

He slides the Styrofoam container in front of me. Suddenly, my stomach flips when I smell the food. It feels like I'm going to throw up right on everything in front of me.. NO! NO! NO! Not now. I take a deep breath and leave the table.

> "Excuse me, I have to go to the
> bathroom."

> "Benny, you think she's, okay?"

> "Yeah, she's fine. You saw her,
> didn't you?"

Upon entering the bathroom, I turn on the water in case they are near the door. It blocks the sound so they won't hear me. I start to vomit. After I throw up my entire breakfast and lunch, I rinse my mouth out. I also wash my face and hands, before returning to the dinner table. I play off my nausea and force myself to eat. The food smells like spoiled milk and bad onions mixed together. I had to hold my breath, chew, and swallow quickly. I almost start to gag. I keep breathing deeply and smiling at them so I won't throw up. As I play tricks on my mind with the food, I hope they don't see my struggle.

> "Is it good, Punkin?"

> "Yeah, Uncle B, it's my favorite right?"

I swallow hard, smile, and begin to silently pray. *"Lord, help me eat some of this food and keep it down in front of them. Just breathe and take a bite. Breathe and take a bite."* I ask the Lord.

> "Jazmyn, if you're done, clear
> your area please, and make sure
> you clean the kitchen."

> "But there's nothing to clean.
> We didn't eat off plates and
> you didn't cook, Auntie."

Auntie ignores my rebuttal and continues with orders.

> "Wipe off the counters, wipe
> the table and sweep the floor.
> Your Uncle and I are almost
> done eating. You will need
> to put away the food too."

I can't stand her! She didn't even cook. Why did I have to do anything? I can just throw away the empty containers, put away the food and be done!

> "Can you let me know when
> you're done, and I will come
> back to *clean the kitchen?"*

> "No, we are almost done. You can start
> on the countertops and get the broom
> going. By the time that's done, we
> will be finished."

I roll my eyes and escape to the bathroom. Uncle Benny married her? Whyyyy! I'll stay in the bathroom as long as I can. I hope they'll be in bed once I leave here. I soon discover that ten minutes in the bathroom isn't long enough. As I get back to the kitchen, I see that Auntie Rachel is still here.

"What's your problem girl?
Why do you keep going to the
bathroom and staying so long?"

"I ate something at school.
My stomach has been hurting
all day."

She turns and walks out without a word. I wipe everything up, clean the kitchen, take my bath, and off to bed. I fall asleep as soon as my head hit the pillow. I immediately start dreaming a recurring dream that I've had since the accident. *I'm lookin' out my bedroom window, wearing white pajamas. As I sit up in my bed, I realized that it's my old bedroom. I smile.*
Seeing my old room made me happy. I opened my door to leave. Next, I fall into a hospital bed. I ask myself, Where are my parents? Why is Uncle Benny and Auntie Rachel here? She looks like she's been crying. I blink about a thousand times trying to clear things up. Instantly, I'm in the back seat of our family car. Daddy is driving and Mommy is in the passenger seat rubbing her pregnant belly. We had just left a beautiful dinner celebration. Then, I hear a loud screech. A car comes speeding through a red light at the intersection and hit us. My seatbelt tightens across my chest. All I hear is shattering glass all around me.

The car flips and lands on its side. I begin to cough from the smoke that invades our car. My father's head is lodged into the shattered car door window and my mother isn't here anymore. The car begins to violently rock back and forth. I can't move. I can't see the other car. I scream, "Aahhhhhh!!

"Punkin! Punkin! Wake up baby!
You are having a bad dream."

Uncle Benny speaks softly. I open my eyes and jump into his arms, crying.

"Heyyyyy, what's going on?"

He asks, hugging me tightly. He pulls back from me and tries to look into my eyes, but I have my hands covering them.

"Was it that dream you told
me about?"

I shake my head yes. This wasn't the first time I woke up like this. I tell him the entire dream, but I wasn't forthright about when the dreams started. I tell him that they started a few days ago. Actually, I've had the same dream every night for two months.

"Look, Punkin, try to get some
sleep. We can talk about it tomorrow.
You have to get up early for school."

He tucks me in like I was ten. Surprisingly, I like it. It makes me feel like his special little girl. I feel so safe with Uncle. After tucking the covers up around my neck, he gives me a loving bearded fuzzy kiss and leaves my room. I close my eyes and wait for my sleep to come back. I can still hear the loud screeeeechhhh, boom, bang and shattered glass from the cars hitting. I put my hand on my stomach. Is there really a baby growing inside me? I yawn and fall fast asleep.

Chapter Three

Ughh!! The cafeteria still has that musty breakfast stench that lingers in the morning air. I hold my breath with each step I take on campus. My stomach is bubbling like it's about to erupt. I hate the volcanic eruption feeling. There are so many things I am clueless about when it comes to being pregnant. Such as being sleepy all the time and eating for two. Also, skipping breakfast is a huge no-no. I watched my momma closely, but she always had a lot of energy and never talked about any problems. I never even saw her get sick. I run to the bathroom, push the door so hard it slams into the wall, and frantically search for an empty stall. It's open. I cover my mouth as I enter. Oooooo, weeeeee! I just made it and it's all going in the toilet. I'll be glad when it stops. Talking about a lava flow. Thank God I'm still in the stall. Ok, it's time to leave this place. It's really sad, but the smell of burning grease over the musty smell is drawing me to the cafeteria. I really should not skip breakfast. Like I said before, I'm eating for two.

Once inside the cafeteria, the smell wasn't so bad. I find it to be very quiet. I mostly hear plastic being ripped from the muffin wrappers and kids whispering like it's a church. I don't want anyone to see me getting this free breakfast because they would think I'm a poor girl with no food at home.

The lunch lady gives me this delicious smelling food. It's a sausage sandwich with an unmelted slice of cheese, a hard blueberry muffin, a carton of milk and carton of orange juice. I see a seat with no one near it. Solitude is my new thing. I sit and begin to remove that nasty cold cheese. I start to eat, and to my surprise, I like it. While eating, Mimi comes in the cafeteria looking for me. I'm stuffing my face like a hungry bear.

"Hey girl, I couldn't believe what I read the text you sent me. In the caf! Really? Why are you eating that po folk's food?"

"I feel so sick. I googled Morning Sickness. It says sometimes you have to eat to feel better. You should try this. It's good. I'm gonna get more before the bell rings."

I tell her as I get up to go for more.

"Hey, you going to Malik's today after school?"

Mimi yells as I walk away to get more food.

"I think so!"

"You gonna tell him?"

She asks when I come back to the table.

"I think so."

While eating my second helping, our friend Cali walks over to us. She sits at our table.

"Hey girlies."

"Hey Cali."

We say in unison. Cali leans over to us like she has a secret.

"Mimi and Jazzy let me tell you
what I heard. Girl, I heard.
Destiny Monroe has amnesia.
Jessica said she called her
yesterday when she was leaving
CVS. Destiny was about to give her
some juicy gossip. Next thing she
heard was Bingggg! Baannnng! Splatttt!
Muffled sounds, static and the phone
went dead. According to Jessica,
Destiny's mom said she suffers from
amnesia. Apparently, she wasn't paying
attention when she left CVS and
bumped her head on a light pole. She
doesn't remember anyone or anything.
Can you believe it?

Mimi and I look at each other. I answer.

"Wow serious? That's terrible."

Mimi says, "Yeah that's horrible."

We are not trying to be sincere, but our fake nonchalant response is sincere enough for Cali. We are so relieved that news of my pregnancy will not be on Destiny's You Tube Channel. The bell rings and it's time to go to class. There is so much on my mind it's going to be difficult to focus today. At the forefront is Malik. His attitude is so volatile. There's no telling how he will respond. Do I tell him this early in the day that I'm pregnant? Close behind that thought is how to get through school without getting sick. Sometimes I want to throw up. Sometimes I want to eat pork chops and watermelon together. Not too far from that is how do I stay awake in class? Man! Teenage pregnancy is madness, so much to do. So much to hide. So much to eventually reveal. Oh yeah, I also have to tell my aunt and uncle too. Lord, please help me. The ten minute bell rings.

First Period is math class. I'm awake and not nauseous, but those numbers don't make any sense right now. The only number I like is seven. In seven minutes, I can leave for second period.

Second Period is my English class and its rough. Every time the teacher turns her back, I fall fast asleep. I hope that I don't drool or snore as that would be embarrassing.

Third Period, health class is even worse than second period. I have to excuse myself. I leave my desk to walk over to Mr. Harrison.

> "Morning sir, may I have a pass
> to the restroom?"

He looks at me and says,

> "How come you didn't go to the
> restroom between classes, that's
> what passing period is for."

> "Mr. Harrison, I didn't have to go
> then. I really need to go now."

Hesitantly, he pulls out a hall pass slip and signs it.

> "Hurry back."

I take it and run to the restroom. Upon entering the stall,
I begin to throw up one barf after another.

Fourth Period I'm free. I don't have a class and lunch follows.
It's a good thing that I don't have a fourth period, because I'm
going to need that period and lunch to throw up. Mimi sends
a text.

> *Mimi - Hey girl! Where you at?*
> *Me -   I'm in the bathroom throwing*
> *up. Is it lunchtime yet?*
> *Mimi -Jazzy, lunch is almost over.*
> *I'm coming to get you.*
> *Me -   Okay. I'm in the one by*
> *Mr. Harrison's class.*

Fifth Period is my Spanish class, a subject I can do without.
If I was not so weak from throwing up the last two periods, I
would skip this class and wait outside my sixth period class.
Now this is funny. Today, I actually understand what's going
on in here. I don't feel tired or sleepy either, just weak.

Sixth Period is my elective, Sewing. This will come in handy as a mother. I can make my baby's clothes. I really like this class. I feel much better now. Maybe because I know that school is almost out. Wow! What is that noise? Boom! Boom! Boom! Boom! I hear nothing but static, misguided bass. Boom! I look out the window and see Malik hanging out his brother's car. I never should have given him the location of my last period class.

"Jazz! Jazzay!"

Malik yells out the car window. I'm completely and instantly embarrassed. He's so ignorant yelling to me outside the car window like that. Have some class Malik, if he waits five minutes, school will be out. I drop my head. I want to sink deep down under my sewing table. Mrs. Bryant walks over to me. She rubs my back and says,

"That'll be it for today! You can leave.
Is everything okay?"

"Yes, Mrs. Bryant. He has life skill issues."

She laughs and walks away. I wonder how she knew that he was calling me. Maybe the look of embarrassment on my face said more than I thought or the fact that he yelled my name. I gather my things and head toward the door. I take several steps down the hall and the bell rings. Once outside I hear Malik yelling,

"Bae! come on! I came to get you!"

I walk over to the car. His brother, Omar, is driving. He's mean. He never smiles or speaks. His silence scares me.

I get in the back seat and Omar burns rubber in the streets, screeeeech! He smashes the accelerator like a drag car racer. Malik begins to speak.

> "I wanted to surprise you, so you
> didn't have to walk to my house."

Malik was yelling over the music from the front seat. I don't answer because the music was too loud and I'm nervous because Omar is speeding as usual.

Malik is a senior at our school. Well, he was until he dropped out about two months ago. He said he didn't need school. He can make a lot of money working for his brother. For some reason he has not figured out that he'll be making a lot of dirty money. It's risky, violent, deadly and one hundred percent illegal. Omar is nothing more than a drug dealer. Malik believes this is the best way to give me the three things he promised. One, an apartment for us to live in. Two, we would get married. Three, I could go to college to get my degree. I really love him and pray that he will keep his promises, but selling drugs is not the way. We arrive and enter the house.

> "Hi, Ms. Miller."

I say to Big Mama upon entering.

> "Hey, baby, how you doin?"

Big Mama says to me.

> "I'm fine Big Mama."

Malik just walks straight to his room and doesn't even speak.
Omar sits on the couch and changes the TV from Big Mama's
show to whatever he wants to watch. He is so disrespectful. I
follow Malik to his room like a little puppy.

Upon entering the room, he immediately grabs me by the
waist, pulls me close and simultaneously closes the door with
his foot.

> "Come here baby I missed you."

He whispers and kisses me. I put my arms around his neck and
lean in to kiss him back. It feels so good being close to him.
I feel warm inside. Suddenly, I jump back. It interrupts the
whole mood.

> "Hey! Boo, what's going on? You okay?"

Malik says looking deep in my eyes as he speaks softly.

> "Oh nothing, I have to go to the
> bathroom."

I knew that when I entered his house I would have to go
badly. I'm feeling nauseous once again, but I must control it. If
I lay on his bed, I won't think about feeling sick anymore. I'm
also a little sleepy. When I walk back into the room, Malik is
already on the bed watching TV. He saves me a little space on
the edge to lay next to him.

"Come on baby, I saved you some
room so you can lay next to me. I
just want to feel you close to me.
We can watch TV. I promise, I
won't try anything."

"Okay,"

I say and happily lay down.

"Baby, you've gained some weight.
I thought I gave you enough room."

Malik never leaves me enough as he jokes before we doze off.
When I wake up, it is dark. I panic. Uncle Benny and Auntie
Rachel are gonna kill me for being late. My heart is beating
fast as I jump up and look for my jacket. As I put it on, I begin
to feel a little dizzy and lose my balance. I fall.

"Malik! Malik! Wake up! I think
I've passed my curfew. They are
going to kill me!"

I yell from the floor. I begin to put my tennis shoes on.

"Huh…what are you talking about?"

Malik says with his eyes still closed. I stand up and punch him
in the side.

"MALIK!" I yell.

"What!"

He shoots straight up in the bed rubbing his side.

34

"Jazz, what!"

I am so mad. I can't believe he let me sleep so long. I grab my backpack and leave his room as quickly as possible.

"Jazz, wait!"

Malik is trying to get up to find his slides.

"Big Mama! Don't let Jazz leave!"

He yells from the room. By the time he comes out of his room, I'm halfway across the lawn. I can't wait for him to wake up and ask me fifty questions when I have to go home. I already know I am in trouble when I get there. I can hear him speaking to big Mama.

"Big Mama did you hear me?"

Malik speaks to his grandmother with disrespect.

"Are you talking to me, boy?"

Big Mama doesn't take her eyes off her TV show. Malik didn't answer.

"I SAID ARE YOU TALKING
TO ME?"

Big Mama doesn't let much slide past her. She takes her eyes off her show and looks directly into Malik's eyes.

"Come on ova here and sit wit me.

I need ta talk to you."

Big Mama's stern tone makes him nervous. He never likes it when she says that she needs to talk to him. He obeys as he sits far away at the corner of the couch.

> "Son, I don't know what you doin wit yo life, but you messin' up that gal's life. She bin comin' ova here fo mo than a yeeea now and she seems ta be here mo and mo. I remema she use ta say she had ta leave cause she had homework. Now, I ain't heard you or her say nothin' for a while. There somethin'else I notice. She's puttin' on some weight. She pregnant? Is she? I see her wearing big ole sweatshirts. This always a sign when dem lil ones get pregnant. I can see."

> "Big Mama, no, she ain't pregnant."

> "I hope you usin' some kinna protection cause you ain't got no bidness wit no baby. You can't get up an go to school no mo. I don unnastand you, but you will pay for all this mess. God don like ugly. You followin' Omar's footsteps, so I will say it again. Be careful with that lil gal of yours, watch it. Don't mess her up. She smart, pretty and wonts to go to college. She tol me that many a time."

"I ain't stupid. I know."

Malik spits on the floor in the house. Big Mama picks up her book and throws it at his head. It smacks him on the side of his face.

"What the . . . !"

Malik responds.

"Watch yo mouf."

She cuts him off before he can finish.

"Boy, I done tol you no cussin in
my presence. Get out ma face
befo I thro somethin else at you."

Big Mama yelled. As he stands he mumbles.

"Sorry, Big Mama, but I didn't
use a curse word."

"GET OUTTA HERE NOW!"

I hear Big Moma several blocks away yelling at Malik. He's grown close to his grandma, but he is feelin' himself since he's been dealing drugs with Omar. I hate that, but I love him. So, I guess I have to deal with it. Especially since he'll be my baby's daddy. When I get home, I see that the light is on in the family room. I was gonna sneak through my bedroom window, but I decided to walk right in the front door. Uncle Benny is sitting in his favorite chair, but I don't see Auntie Rachel.

"Hey, Punkin!"

Uncle Bennie says. Always pleasant.

"Hey Uncle B."

I say as I walk past him to my room. When I get into my room, I have a bunch of clothes on my bed and a note from "The Aunt."

Jazmyn
These are all the clothes I found in various spots around the house and all over your room. They need to be washed and put away. I'm sure they aren't clean. Get it done tonight. There are no maids here!
Thank you,
Aunt Rachel

Oh boy! What is this a formal letter? Signing thank you and Aunt Rachel. She didn't have to put all of that on there. She's always trying to be proper, but she's fake. This pile is very big. There's no way that I have all these clothes all over the house. She's always making stuff up and blaming me. I keep my stuff in my room. I wonder if she was in my room snooping around. Before I do anything, I want to check my messages on my Instagram account. I saw something. She can wait with this washing stuff. Oh, a message from a guy named Sexysean. I look through his page. He is so fine, but he looks a little old. He looks like he's out of school. He has a black Camaro with tinted windows. Nice car. His pictures are cool. On one picture he is wearing blue jeans, a pair of blue and black Jordans and a black t-shirt with *Just Do It* written on it. Sexysean seems tall in the picture. Another one of the pictures has a close-up of his face. Those light brown eyes on his dark brown skin looks absolutely dreamy. Why does it look like he's looking at me?

His message said, *"Hey cutie, your pictures look fly. I wanna get to know you. Why don't you drop me a text or DM."* I read it again. Malik would be so mad if he knew I were talking to another dude. How would he find out? I love him, but this dude is cute with a car. Malik is still walking and begging friends for rides. It won't hurt to have a friend. *I message him.*

> *Hey, what do you wanna know about me?*

Before I receive an answer, let me put this phone down. I need to put some clothes in the wash before the crazy lady comes in and says something to me. After placing clothes in the laundry basket, I walk over to my Uncle and ask.

> "Uncle Benny, where is Auntie Rachel?"

> "She went out for a bit. She will be back in a while. Did you get her note?"

He never takes his eyes off the TV.

> "Can I ask you another question, Uncle?"

> "Sure."

He turns the TV off and gives me his full attention.

> "Why was she snooping in my room?"

> "Hey, I don't get in y'alls stuff. You have to ask her. She was fussing about you and your clothes being everywhere."

He always tries to play the mediator between us.

He knows how she treats me, but I do realize that's his wife. I think Uncle Benny is just happy I'm in the house with him. I hear him talking to Auntie Rachel sometimes about going a little easier on me, but she would always have a reason why she needed to stay strict with me.

"I don't have clothes all over the place. Where did she get all of this from?"

"Punkin, I told you. I don't know."

I went to the laundry room and started my wash. I need to talk to Mimi to see what she's doing. I have to tell her about Malik too. As I enter my room, my phone is ringing. It's Mimi.

"Hey, girl, I was about to call you."

"I felt the vibe. You know that best friend thing, so I called you."

Mimi laughs.

"Oh, whatever girl. What's up wichu?"

"Nothing, I just finished my homework."

"Girl, I just got home."

She begins to speak but I didn't hear her. I was sitting on my bed looking around. There was laundry being done and homework to be done, but I wanted to talk to Mimi first. No one ever checked me about my homework. Uncle B and Auntie Rachel probably knew, if I didn't do anything else, I would get my homework done. Next thing I know I hear Mimi.

"Wait, from where? Not Malik's?"

Mimi is surprised.

"Yeah, he was all over me when
I got there. He was talkin' bout he
missed me. I was like, what is really
going on. Then he started kissin'
me. I was scared he would feel
my little belly bump, so I ran to the
bathroom."

Mimi started laughing with me.

"You aren't really showing. It looks
like you gained a little weight, but
you are so small nobody can see it.
So, when are you going to tell him?"

"I don't know. I fell asleep over there
and woke up past my curfew. Girl,
every time I go to sleep it's so good.
I don't know what it is. I was
knocked out; and when I woke up,
it was dark. I was in panic mode
and tried to wake stupid Malik up.
He was all slow, so I ran out of the
house. He was callin' me back. I
kept going. I don't like him right
now, Mimi."

"Why not?"

"Because I have to tell him I'm
pregnant and I don't know how
he's going to react. I want him
to be excited like me. Oh! Wait!
I met a dude on Instagram. He is
so cute."

Mimi gets quiet for a minute. I don't know what she is doing
because it's so quiet. Is she off the phone?

"Mimi, you there, girl?"

"I'm here, I'm trying to figure
out how you meetin' dudes on
Instagram. You are pregnant
and in love with Malik.
Again, why are you scared of
telling Malik?"

"Who said I was scared?"

"Jazzy, I know you. You act like
you are scared of something.
Just tell the dude you are having
his baby. You said you love him
and all that. He loves you. So, hey
you are having his baby."

Mimi has some sound advice, but I couldn't tell my best friend
how he acts when he's mad. She doesn't know what he does
to me.

"Anyway, Sean sent me a message.
He has a blacked-out Camaro.
He looks a little older, but girl
he is fine!"

"You are playing with fire. How
do you know he has a blacked-out
Camaro? Stop messaging him and
tell Malik he is gonna have a baby."

I hear Uncle Benny call me from his favorite chair in the
family room.

"Hey, let me call you back
Uncle B is callin'me."

"Stop talking to the new dude!"

She yells before she hangs up.

"We only text! Bye girl!"

Chapter Four

It's month four of the pregnancy and no one knows a thing, except Mimi. I haven't told Malik because I'm afraid of how he will react. Will he be happy? Or will he get mad and slap me down? I'm too far along to deal with physical abuse. I'm beginning to show a little, so I constantly avoid people as much as possible, specifically Malik. He thinks I'm busy at school trying to finish up strong before the Christmas break. He also thinks he will see me during the break, but the family and I are going to San Francisco.

Every other year we spend the holidays with Auntie Rachel's sister, Auntie Noonie. We go there for Christmas Eve and leave the day after Christmas. We have so much fun there. I really enjoy spending time with the entire family. Auntie Noonie is great, but what kind of name is Noonie? I ask myself. She treats me like family even though we're not. We're related because my uncle married her evil sister. She wants me to call her Auntie Noonie, so, Auntie Noonie it is. She is night and day from Auntie Rachel. Auntie Rachel is the night part and midnight at that. She's jealous because Auntie Noonie is a diva. She's single and doesn't work. She has a big ol' house overlooking the bay. She's pretty and looks like a runway fashion model, very beautiful. Auntie Rachel, on the other hand, is a snotty big nose witch! If I weren't trying to follow Jesus' example, I would take out the "W" and replace it with another letter. She's always turning that nose up at someone too. I always hear Auntie Rachel saying evil things to Auntie Noonie. Just nagging her about petty issues.

Always prying into her business, but Auntie Noonie just ignores her and changes the subject. One day when Auntie Noonie and I were alone I asked,

"Why is she so evil?"

"Baby, your Auntie Rachel has been through a lot. When we were little a man touched her multiple times."

The details were left out so I don't know what he did to her or who he was. I guess I don't need to know. Auntie Rachel has been mean ever since. Auntie Noonie says it's her sister and she loves her no matter what. I love that she continues to have Christmas at her house every other year. Auntie Noonie says, "I understand my sister is in pain. I will always be here for her." Auntie Noonie is so loving to her sister. I, on the other hand, pass on that old evil bat. I don't care what Auntie Noonie says. I don't like her and she doesn't like me.

Anyway, being away from Malik will be nice. I will only text him. I don't want to call him. My goal is to keep my baby bump undetected from everyone this holiday. My baggy sweats and hoodies will hide me perfectly. I will take my favorite throw blanket to wrap up in at all times. It's always cold, so I should be able to stay under the radar. My phone makes a noise. It's Malik.

> *Malik - Hey bae wyd?*
> *Jazzy - Nothing.*
> *Malik - You haven't sent me any pictures.*
> *Jazzy - Send pictures for what?*
> *Malik - I miss you.*
> *Jazzy - I miss you too.*

I can't hardly wait to get away from him. He makes me feel like I have to walk on pins and needles because I don't want to make him mad. He can be set off by anything. Suc as, me talking to a guy or him looking at my phone and sees a text from someone. Malik wants all of my attention. I don't want to talk to him right now.

> *Malik - When can I talk to you.*
> *I wanna hear your voice.*
> *Jazzy - I don't know.*
> *Malik - I'm gonna call you in the morning.*
> *Answer the phone! Your aunt and*
> *uncle should be asleep.*

I shudder at his last text. How does he have me like this? Why am I still with him? He really scares me. Now that I'm pregnant, maybe he will be nicer longer.

> *Jazzy – Okay, I have to go.*
> *Malik – WHY, I'M NOT DONE TALKIN'*
> *Jazzy - Bye Malik.*

I'm done texting him. He's about to get mean because he's not getting his way. I'll be glad when I get to Auntie Noonie's house.

Two weeks later it's Christmas Day. I'm thinking about what I've been through and what lies ahead. My cousin Ricki comes in the room with me. She is a nice distraction. Ricki says,

> "Jazz, you picking up some weight?"

> "Yeah, I've been eating a little more.
> I'm tired of being small. It's hard to
> eat a lot of food though, you know?"

"Your face is getting fuller. Take that
blanket off so I can see your body
and see where else you're gaining
weight."

I think to myself. *Heck no, I'm not getting up.* I stay wrapped
in the blanket perfectly snug, and I am not moving until I go to
bed.

"I'm tired girl, I don't feel like getting up."

"Well, you look good. Keep eating."

We sit in silence and watch TV. I dodge a bullet. We hang out
when I visit, but I am sick a lot and call it the flu so the adults
will leave me alone. Uncle Benny keeps watching me with that
worried look on his face. I try to be social so I don't draw
attention to myself. It's really hard because of the way I
always feel.

Christmas Day is hard because there are so many different
food smells. I feel a little flutter in my stomach while sitting at
the dinner table. I jump and everyone looks at me. I play it off
and say I feel a sharp pain in my back. I make sure it doesn't
look like I am in pain. I really need to walk unnoticed today.
This is my secret until I get back home to figure things out.
I just don't know what that feeling was.

The next day Uncle Benny tells me to pack my stuff. We have
to catch our plane in two hours. Auntie Noonie does not live
that far from the airport, but my Uncle Benny knows that it
takes black families about an hour to say good-bye. That's why
we're leaving so early. I really hate to leave Auntie Noonie.I
love it here. Her house is warm and cozy.

Her fireplace is always lit and the candles are spreading an indescribably pleasant fragrance. It's always clean too. I think she has a "Moonlight Maid" who comes in while everyone is sleeping and cleans. It's a disaster when we go to bed and spotless when we get up.

Uncle Benny says,

> "Punkin' start putting your things in the car. We are leaving in about ten minutes."

> "Okay."

I take my things to Auntie Noonie's car. Inside the house everyone is saying their goodbyes. I'm done with the goodbyes. I stay in the car and wait. Auntie Noonie and Ricki come out to the car.

Ricki says,

> "Bye cousin. Hurry up and come back so we can hang out without these old folk. My mom said you can stay at our house next time."

Uncle B and Auntie Rachel walk up.

> "Hey, hey who you calling old."

Auntie Rachel says.

> "I don't know who she's calling old, cuz I aint hardly old."

Auntie Noonie chimes in. We all laugh and the old folks pile in the car and we head to the airport. The flight is uneventful and as soon as we get home the smell of the house immediately makes me nauseous. I go to my room and lay down. Once again, I fall fast asleep.

Early the next morning, I decided to get dressed to go see Malik. It's time that I tell him about our future blessing. I put on my usual baggy sweats, that aren't so baggy, and hoodie, with my hair pulled in a bun. Surprisingly, I don't feel like I have to throw up. I tell Uncle Benny that I am going to Mimi's house. He never questions me about where I'm going, as long as I tell him something, he's ok. As I leave the house, I see the Lawnboy from school cutting the grass. He's been around doing a lot of chores for Uncle Benny lately. I just saw him two days ago digging in the flower bed. I don't know his real name, but I know he's from school. He looks at me so weird when he's at the house. He hangs with the nerdy kids. I see him looking, but not looking. He's just a freshman so it doesn't matter what he does.

On my walk over to Malik's, I practice what I am going to say. As I go up the walkway, I see Malik's little cousins playing outside in the dirt. I knock on the screen of the barred door.

"Yeaaaaahhhh!"

Big Mama yells from inside.

"It's Jazzy, Big Mama, is Malik here?"

I say through the barred screen door.

"Yeah, baby, come on in, he's in his room."

49

As I walk through, I try not to look at her house dress. She has a big glass jar of ice water on her side table and bbq pork rinds. She doesn't say anything to me as I pass by. His grandmother looks at me like she knows something. She sits in her big chair with her house dress on and her legs wide open showing her white granny panties. Her legs are open because they are too fat to close. I don't think I've seen her in anything else, only those house dresses. They are the old lady house dresses with the two pockets in front with buttons or snaps. Maybe I saw a brand new one once. The others I've seen are so faded the flowers look like they are traced on. I like her. I think we have an understanding. It seems like she likes me. She's cool, to me, but makes me uncomfortable at times. Her eyes seem to bore into my soul. It's almost like she sees my thoughts. Malik's door is closed, so I knock.

"Yo!" He yells from the other side.

He put his phone down quickly like he is hiding something.

"Babe, you didn't call me before
you came over here."

He says looking guilty.

"I didn't think I needed to. Who's
that on the phone?"

"Nobody."

I sit on the bed. I don't like the look on his face.

"So wassup wichu?"

He says, trying to distract me.

"Nothing, you said you wanted
me to come over. Here I am."

I said with no emotion. He gets up and goes to the bathroom
without a word. He leaves his phone on the bed. I pick it up
and look at his text.

> *LeeLee - Malik when can we get*
> *together again?*
> *Malik - Soon, baby girl, soon.*
> *LeeLee -You said you wanted to be*
> *with me.*
> *Malik - I do but I gotta handle some*
> *business first.*

I hear him coming and put the phone down, so he won't catch
me being nosey. I can't believe he is texting Lee Lee again. He
comes into the room and sits next to me. He tries to kiss me.
I turn away.

"Why you actin' so funny?"

"I ain't actin' funny,"

I am so mad at him. Lee Lee is a girl at school he used to mess
with, but it looks like he's talking to her again. She cussed him
out in front of the whole cafeteria one day.

"You act like you gotta attitude.
You not gonna kiss me?
Why you here?"

"Dang, you ain't gotta be mean. Why
are you talking to Lee Lee again?"

"YOU BEEN LOOKIN THOO
MA PHONE AGAIN!"

I stand up and tighten my body to brace myself for what may come next. When he raises his voice there is usually some type of violence next. He grabs my arm and pulls me close to him firmly.

"Let go of me, Malik, that hurts!"

I try to get away. His grip is too tight.

"I TOLD YOU NOT TO MESS
WIT MA PHONE."

I'm afraid. He frowns hard with his forehead. His shoulders come in closer to his neck as his anger rises. I can see it in his eyes too.

"Malik, please let me go. You're
hurting me."

I say, squirming to get out of his grip. I struggle to break free. He tightens his grip. I don't know what he is going do next. Before I can say anything else he throws me against his closet door, I fall and hit my head on the side table next to his bed. There is a loud boom as the table falls over. I lay on the floor grabbing my head. The pain is excruciating.

"My baby."

I whisper as I cry and get off the floor.

"What did you say?"

Malik says, still angry and blocking the doorway.

"Move, Malik!"

I lean in to push him out of the way.

"Jazz, what did you say?"

"Nothin' Malik! Let me go.
I wanna go home."

I start to cry. The door rattles as Big Mama pounds on the door.

"Malik, let that gal go! Open this
door now!"

He didn't move. Malik is so angry he ignores Big Mama's command. Through his clenched teeth and low voice, he says,

"Stop cryin'! Now!"

I wipe my face quickly and suck it up. He slowly opens the door. I think Big Mama scared him. I walk past them both and leave. As I walk home, I can feel my chest about to explode. I don't realize I am holding my breath while taking long strides like my momma always told me to do. This isn't a confident walk though. It is a walk of pain. I can feel hot tears rolling down my cheeks. I stop for a moment and try to breathe. I finally take a deep breath. I'm ready for the scream that follows. It is a bunch of air and a loud shriek. My chest heaves up and down as I sob. I make my way to the curb, sit down, and put my head in my hands. I cry because I am afraid of what Malik could have done. Sitting for a while, I try to calm myself. I begin to daydream.

Suddenly, I'm staring across the street. I thought about the time
Malik got mad at me and pushed me into the wall in his room.
I hit my head on that wall this time. I had a bad headache from
that and a small fingerprint bruise on my shoulder. After he did
it, he started saying he was sorry. He said, "Oh, bae, I'm sorry.
I'm sorry. Please forgive me. Sit down. Are you okay?" I
quietly cry. I wiped the tears from my face and sat on the bed. I
wouldn't look at him. I was mad. How could he do that to me?
He's supposed to love me. "Bae, talk to me. Jay, please don't
cry," he said and kissed me on my lips. I refused to talk to him
though. My shoulder was burning, and my head was
pounding. It hurt so badly in the back. "Malik. I want to leave,"
I said without looking at him. "Jay, don't leave me. Please. I
love you. Just stay and let me hold you." I laid back on his
bed and just closed my eyes, hoping it was just a dream. He
laid behind me, wrapped his arms around me and put his head
close to my head. He kissed the back of my head and kept
apologizing. I didn't feel well. Thinking about that incident
made me forget I'm still sitting on the curb. I finally felt good
enough to start walking home. The whole time I sat on the curb
I could feel my phone vibrating in my back pocket. As I stand,
I look at my phone. I have six notifications from Malik. I
ignore him. How am I going to tell him I am pregnant with his
baby? How? What if he hits me? I gotta figure something out.
Maybe I can go up to Auntie Noonie's house. She's so cool.
She would let me stay and have the baby there. I'll call her as
soon as I get in front of the house. The curb is uncomfortable,
so I head home. I reach the driveway and begin to call Auntie
Noonie.

"Hello? Jazmyn, how are you doing?"

"Hi, Auntie!"

"How are you, honey?"

"I'm fine. I was just thinking about you.
I wanna come to visit."

"Oh, sweetie, you are always welcome
here. You just let me know and I will
have your room ready. Does my sister
know you want to visit me?"

"No, she doesn't. I will talk to her to
see when I can come."

"Are you sure you're okay?
You don't sound like it.
Is something bothering you?"

I hold back my tears. I hope she can't hear me.

"Auntie, I'm fine. I'll call you
when I'm ready to come out
there, okay?"

I want to just hang up.

"Okay baby,"

"Okay, I love you auntie. Bye"

"I love you more. Bye bye."

As I end the call, I am about to walk into the house. I'm going to check my bank account to see how much money I have in there. I'll need some money to buy a plane ticket to Auntie Noonie's. When I get in the house I go straight to my room. Uncle B is not in his chair. It's early afternoon. It's unusual he isn't in his chair watching TV. I pass his room. He and Auntie Rachel are asleep. They never take naps. I am glad they are sleeping so that I can devise a plan.

Once in my room, I get my laptop out and begin to check flights. I'm pretty good at looking for flights because Auntie always made me reserve the tickets to the bay for Christmas. I buy a one-way ticket for thirty dollars. My flight leaves at 9:00am tomorrow morning. I pack everything necessary to stay for three days. If I need to stay longer, I'll figure it out later. Besides, I can only fit three pairs of sweats now anyway.

After I pack my bag, I quietly walk down the hall. I slip outside and place my bag near the big green bush by the driveway. As I turn to walk back in the house, I run smack into Malik.

"Aaahhhh!" I scream.

Malik puts his hand over my mouth and whispers,

"Shhhh, Somebody might hear you."

When he takes his hand down I whisper.

"Why are you here?"

"I need to talk to you; and you won't answer your phone."

"Yeah, because I don't want to talk
to you Malik. Leave me alone."

"I told you I'm sorry and I won't do
it again."

"Malik, I know you won't."

"What's that supposed to mean?"

"I'm agreeing with what you said.
I will also make sure it stays that
way."

"Jazz what are you talking about?"

"Malik it's over."

Malik freezes. Then speaks.

"What did you say? It's over?
You can't quit me!"

"I just did."

I walk away. He grabs my arm. Here we go again.

"Malik! I will yell so loud that
all my neighbors, including my
uncle and aunt will hear me. Let
me go and you go home."

"Jazzy, you can't quit me.
I love you."

"Let me go, and you go home
please, before I scream for my
uncle."

He releases his grip. Out of nowhere, Lawnboy rolls up on his
bike.

"Hey is everything okay, Jazmyn?"

"What's it to you nerd boy?"

Malik interrupts.

"Everything is fine, he's just leaving.
What are you doing here?"

"I need to speak with your uncle.
Can you go get him, please?"

I pause for a minute and begin to check him out. He's really a
very handsome youngman. He's a freshman with a baby face,
smooth caramel skin and curly hair. His hair is curly on top
and lays flat and close on the sides of his head. I think they call
that a fade. He has on an Adidas hoodie, jeans that look like
they are flooding, but I can't tell for sure on his bike, and white
Air Force Ones. Oh my gosh, Lawnboy is taller than Malik!
Wow, I'm sure he doesn't like that. There is something a little
cute about Lawnboy on a bike with black rimmed glasses and
a helmet.

"Okay, let me go get him."

As I walk away Malik and Lawnboy stare at one another. I go
in the house and don't go directly to Uncle Benny.

I look out the window and see them having words, but not like they are gonna fight. Lawnboy left on his bike one way and Malik walked off the opposite way. He yells out,

> "You will pay for this Jazmyn Jackson!
> You will pay!"

Whatever Malik, I say to myself. That Lawnboy is really something. I don't know if he really wanted to talk to Uncle Benny or not, but whatever his intentions were, he saved me from Malik with his cute self.

Chapter Five

Malik's last words shook me a little. I hope he doesn't haunt me or try to hurt me. Standing in my room, I look around and think about what my next steps will be. I start to put my school stuff together.

Buzz! Buzzzzz! While lying around to ponder my next move, Mimi interrupts my thoughts with a text.

Mimi - Hey, Jazz.

Jazzy - Mimi girl, whatchu doing?

Mimi - Nothin'

Jazzy - Look! I'm goin' out of town today.

Mimi - Where are you goin'?

Jazzy - I don't wanna tell you cuz I don't wanna get you in trouble for knowing anything. I just wanted to tell you I won't be at school. Don't look for me.

Mimi - Don't tell me you are going somewhere with that old man

Jazzy - He ain't an old man. I'm not going to tell you.

Mimi - Well, where are you goin'?

Jazzy - Look, I will let you know when I get there. Okay?

Mimi - Why? Are you running away? What happened? Did you tell Malik?

> *Jazzy - I just need to go think. No, I*
> *didn't tell him yet. I need space.*
> *I will text you.*

I put my phone on the bed. I grab my prenatal pills and throw them in my backpack. I'm sure they are helping my baby. Ever since I confirmed the pregnancy, I've been taking them daily. I feel more movement. Auntie Noonie is usually home most of the day. I will hang in the airport until she can pick me up. I put the Uber app on my phone just in case she can't pick me up. Living with Auntie Noonie will be perfect. I won't have to deal with anyone, especially Malik. Uncle Benny might be a little upset, but Auntie Rachel probably won't even know I'm gone. I begin to text Sean for my ride.

> *Jazzy – Hey Sean wassup?*

I wait for a response. Sean usually answers quickly. It has already been at least fifteen minutes and no answer. Finally!!!

> *Sean – Hey Jazzy.*
> *Jazzy – Can you do me a favor?*
> *I need a ride to the*
> *airport. Can you take*
> *me?*

Again, I wait a good fifteen to twenty minutes for his response. He's a jerk. Why do I have to wait so long for a simple response? I throw the phone on the bed and decide to clean up anything laying around in my room. I want it spotless before I leave.

> *Sean – Sorry, I can't. I have to work.*
> *Jazzy –Fine, you're always at work.*

He is a loser, nice to talk to, but a loser! I'll get a car to pick me up at 7-Eleven across the street from the school.

> *Sean – Where are you going?*
> *Don't you have school?*
> *Jazzy –I have to take a quick*
> *trip somewhere.*
> *Sean – Jazzy, you told me you*
> *were pregnant. Are you*
> *sure you should be*
> *traveling?*
> *Jazzy - I have to get away for a bit.*
> *I need some space to think.*
> *Sean – Do you have a bank account?*
> *I can send you money to get a*
> *car to the airport.*
> *Jazzy – Sean that's so sweet. I have an*
> *app you can send me the money on.*

I don't want to give him any personal information because I don't know him that well. My uncle always told me to keep my bank account and social security number private. He can send money to my getmoneyapp account.

> *Sean – Are you going to give me the*
> *information?*
> *Jazzy – Yes if you give me a chance.*
> *It's the getmoney app and*
> *my name is JJJazzz.*
> *Sean – Okay I will send the money*
> *now. You will let me know*
> *when you get where you*
> *are going right?*

*Jazzy –I will. Thank you so much
Sean, you're the best.
Sean – You're welcome. Please stay
in touch.
Jazzy –Okay.*

I hear a soft knock on the door.

"Come in."

"Hey, ladybug. You doing, okay? You've
been so quiet lately. I was wondering
if anything was going on? Are you upset
with us about anything?"

He says with a concerned look on his face.

"Uncle Benny, I'm fine," as I sit on the bed.

He sits next to me.

"Okay, because I don't want my ladybug
upset and not wanting to talk to me. You
know you can talk to me about anything."

He says as he puts his arm around me. I notice his arm isn't
as big and strong as it used to be. It seems a little thin. When I
look in his eyes, he looks a little weak. He lost some weight. I
don't know why I haven't noticed that before.

"Uncle Benny, are you okay?
You don't look so good."

"Ladybug, I'm fine. I just need a little
rest. Your aunt and I have been runnin'
around a little too much. I just need
to go to bed. I'm glad you are okay.
I love you."

We hug, but now I feel bad that I'm running away. Sadly, there's no turning back. I'm leaving for my baby's safety and mines too. No one will understand.

"Uncle Benny, I love you so much
you are my most favoritest uncle
in the whole wide world." I kiss
his cheek and he leaves my room.

Evil Auntie Rachel never came into my room much. If she did, it was only to complain or throw a bunch of junk on my bed or tell me to do something. I really feel she doesn't want me here. It's like I'm in her way. I feel like I've been a burden to her ever since I got here. They picked me up at the hospital, after the accident. She looked at me like the accident was my fault. Turning her nose up at me all the way here. She never had any compassion or comforting words for me. All she ever did was ramble off rules from the hospital until now. Uncle Benny was always the one to console me. She never gave me a chance to know her. It wasn't like I saw her all the time when my parents were alive. I never even spent the night over their house. In fact, I saw Uncle Benny quite often. He would come over to our house all the time and visit, alone. I would hear my mom ask about her, only out of courtesy, but that was the extent of my knowledge regarding her. Well, I had a little more information about her. My mother called her an "Anti-social Weirdo." Now that I live with her, I agree.

She's not that anti-social though. She's always doing things with her friends. She is usually the life of the party with them; but with me, she's an evil good for nothing witch. Again, if I weren't trying to love Jesus, I would drop the letter 'W' and replace it with a 'B'. Speaking of 'B's my baby bump is really getting big. There's a real person inside me. I have to rub it, but I'm always scared I might hurt my internal organs or something. I just can't believe I'm going to be a mother. I know if my mother knew this, she would be so disappointed with me. Just the thought of my mom being upset with me makes me sad. Tears roll down my cheek. *"I'm sorry, mommy."* I whisper. I quietly cry for what my mother would think. I need to get out of this house because I don't wanna deal with Auntie Rachel fussing at me or kicking me out. This would only give her more reason to hate me. I scan the room and see that all my bags are in place. I look at my phone and discover that Malik has sent multiple text messages. He is blowing up my phone. I don't want to talk to him. He wants to apologize for the way he acted. Once again he'll say he's sorry and will never put his hands on me. That will last for a few days. Then suddenly, I'll be looking up at him from the floor. Once he got mad because my phone went off while we were kissing. He accused me of cheating. My phone was in my backpack. He grabbed it, ripped it open and dumped all my stuff out. He turned it upside down and threw my books and stuff all over his room looking for my phone. When I tried to grab my stuff, he pushed me to the floor.

> "You bet not let me find out you
> are talking to anotha dude!"

I slid into the corner, held my knees close and begin to cry and shake. I had no idea what he would do next.

Once he got my phone, he saw it was locked with my password and threw it at my head.

"OPEN IT!!"

I ducked and tried to get out of the room. I was crawling quickly to the door. Then suddenly something changed in him.

"Baby, baby, baby, wait. Come on, get up. I'm sorry. I didn't mean to scare you. Are you okay?"

He was quiet and sweet now. He pulled me close to him and hugged me tightly. He kept saying he was sorry over and over again. Finally, he let me go, and began to pick up my stuff that fell out of my backpack. He gently placed them back inside. I looked around for my phone. It was behind a chair. When I picked it up, I see cracks on the screen. It looks like a spider web. Staring at it, I began to cry again. He turned around to see why I was crying. I just turned my phone screen to him and got off the floor to get my backpack.

"Baby, I promise I'll get it fixed for you."

"You don't have to."

I wiped my eyes. Putting my backpack down I decided to go to the bathroom to check my face. I couldn't go home looking like I had been crying. In the bathroom, I studied my face closely. Splashing warm water on it, I felt confused. I haven't seen him act like this since he pushed me down for looking at his phone. I was scared, but I love him. I love him so much, and deep down inside his foolish interior, he may love me.

"Jay, you, okay?"

"Malik, why you whispering through the door? You weird."

I heard a little voice say.

"Shut up, Mookie. Get outta here!"

I slowly opened the door.

"I'm fine. I need to go home."

I want to get my belongings and go. I walk past him to his room and grab my backpack. He is walking behind me. I feel a tug on my backpack as I put my arm in.

"Jay, I don't want you to leave. Man, I'm sorry. I'm really, really sorry. I love you."

"Malik, I need to go, okay?"

He gently turned my face to his and kissed me. I didn't kiss back. I wanted to leave.

"Malik, I have to go, okay?"

I insisted, holding back the tears. He fell to the bed and had his head down acting like his feelings were hurt. I was mad. I just walked out and left him sitting there looking stupid. I didn't care.

I can't hardly wait to leave. I'll be much better once I'm away. But I'm always better once I'm away from him. Away from the pain. Away from the violence. Away from numerous incidents. Away from avoiding close calls to avoid bodily harm. Away from painful tears welling up in my eyes to crash down on a shattered heart like waves upon a sandy floor. So, Malik will get upset regardless. I want to go to Auntie Noonie's and figure my life out. I close my eyes and go to sleep. Suddenly, I am so tired and feel so fat. I smell coffee. That means Auntie is up. I have to get dress like I'm going to school. I look at my belly while getting dressed, it looks huge. Oh my! I'm showing for real. After combing my hair, I leave my room. I have to walk past Auntie, but that shouldn't be hard. I look like I'm going to school. I don't want to raise any suspicion. I hope Uncle B isn't with her. He already suspects something. That's why he came in my room this morning. I can tell by the way he looks at me. That's something special about our relationship we can tell when one of us is stressed about something or in deep thought about an issue. I just can't talk to him because he will tell Auntie Meany. When I pass the kitchen, I hear Auntie call my name.

> "Uhhhh, Jazmyn, is that you?
> I made you some breakfast."

I stop and turn around so she won't say I am being rude.

> "Auntie, I'm not hungry right
> now. Thank you."

> "You need breakfast," She insists.

I head for the door and roll my eyes so she doesn't see me. One minute she's being nice and the next she's being a nasty you know what.

Thank you, Jesus for not letting me use that 'B' word.

"I'm good. I'm running late for school."

I say and walk out of the door. I can still hear her talking.

Once outside, I sneak quietly to the side of the house, grab my bag and hope no one will look out of the window or hear me in the bushes. I'm so glad we are only two houses from the corner. It only takes two seconds to get around the block. I notice the smell of bacon coming from someone's house and it smells good too. I'm surprised because that smell usually makes me sick. Maybe I should have stayed to eat. My baby kicks me. Ok, ok, I'll get us something to eat. Well, I guess that was a kick for food. It feels like a flutter. Like fish swimming in my stomach. I stop and wait until it goes away. Once it stops, I start walking to 7-11 to meet my car. Sexysean is so sweet for ordering a car since he can't take me. Sometimes, I think I like him because he is willing to do anything for me. I didn't tell him much about Malik and he doesn't ask. I'm a little concerned, but not too much. He's a grown man. He doesn't have time for little kids and I'm going to be a mom. I need a mature guy. As I walk in the parking lot the driver drives in. I pull up the app to confirm the driver that Sean sent.

"So, pretty girl, you are headed for the airport, correct?"

The driver asks.

"Is your name Javier?"

I ask to verify the driver.

"Yes ma'am."

"Okay, yes please, I'm going to LAX."

He drives me very rapidly to Southwest Airlines curbside. As he pulls up to the curb, I take a moment to thank Javier. He gets out, opens my door and retrieves my bags from the trunk. While I'm pulling the handle up on my bag, I see a car pass me and the passenger looks just like Malik. Why would he be at the airport? My bag starts to roll away. My attention is redirected to Javier.

"Thank you, Javier, for the ride."

I say as I walk towards the terminal entrance.

"You're welcome, Miss Jazmyn."

As I approach the gate, I look around and see rows of black seats connected. I look for a place to sit alone. An announcement is spoken over the intercom.

"Ladies and Gentlemen, welcome to flight 1222 with service to San Francisco. In just a few moments we will be boarding. Please take a moment to review your boarding pass to verify your seat assignment to ensure that you board with your proper boarding group."

I dig in my backpack to find my boarding pass. I panic be cause I can't feel it. Then I realize it's in my hoodie pocket. Whew, I'm ready to board the plane. I text Sean, before boarding starts, to let him know I made it okay.

*Me – Hey Sean, I made it to the gate.
Thanks again for the ride.*

*Sean – So glad you made it to the
airport. Now where are you
going?*

*Me - I'm just going to my aunt's
house to figure some things
out.*

*Sean - Things like what? I know you
said something about a
boyfriend. Is he one of the
things that you need to figure
out?*

*Me – Well kind of. I don't want to be
his girlfriend anymore though.*

S ean– What happened?

*Me –Long story, I will text later. I
need to get ready to board my
flight.*

I board the flight and go straight to sleep. The flight was over
in seconds. Well, it felt that way. I don't remember any part
of the flight. What I do remember is someone shaking me to
wake up and get off the plane. I turn my phone back on and see
messages from Malik.

Malik - Jazz call me. I want to talk.

*Malik - I need to talk to you please
call me.*

*Malik - Jazz okay so you don't wanna
hit me back. I saw you get in
that car this morning and
I followed you to the airport.
You looked right at me when
I passed by.*

Jazzy - Okay Malik.

I call Auntie Noonie.

"Hi Auntie Noonie! I'm here."

I pause to hear her response.

"Yes, I made it. I guess it was okay.
I slept all the way here. Okay,
okay, huh? Mhmm! Alright, see
you soon. Bye."

We briefly exchange pleasant verbage and she tells me how to take BART to her house. The train ride is cool. I am not scared like I thought I would be. I kept my bags close to me like she instructed. What I can't figure out is why she didn't come to get me? I didn't know the train would be my ride. Whatever, when I exit the station, her little Red Porsche SUV is parked at the curb waiting for me. She gets out to give me a hug.

"Hey, little lady. How are you?"

"I'm fine. How are you?"

"I'm so happy to see you.".

I throw my suitcase in the back, hop in the car, and notice how quiet Auntie is. She doesn't live far. In ten minutes we are in the hills pulling into her driveway. Everything seems to be moving fast. Once in the house, she tells me where to place my things.

"Get your things, put them in your room
and meet me in the kitchen, Love."

She doesn't sound all bubbly like normal. I am getting
worried. Maybe this isn't the best place to figure things out.
Since there is one suitcase and one backpack, I put it on the
bed and join her downstairs. She sits at the table with a cup of
coffee. I can see the steam coming from the cup. Both of her
hands are cupped around it and she is looking out the
window at her beautiful lush green backyard. Auntie Noonie
loves plants and flowers. In one corner it's like a mini botani-
cal garden with different kinds of flowers, a bridge with a little
pond under it, and a few small trees. It is so beautiful. On the
otherside, there is a patio with exotic patio furniture, a fire pit
and a built in BBQ grill. I sit on the edge of the dinette chair
thinking this will be a quick conversation because I am sleepy.

> "Love, I want to know why you wanted
> to come here? What's going on?"

Auntie says calmly. I'm quiet and I look down at the table.
I feel tears burning the back of my eyes. Holding them back is
hard. I take a deep breath before I start.

> "I know you had school today. I'm certain
> Rachel doesn't know you are here. When
> you called, I decided not to ask too many
> questions because I wanted to see you. I
> wanted to look you in your face and see
> what's going on. You know, your Auntie
> ain't no fool. I can see you have put on
> some weight since you were here last
> month for Christmas. Love, are you
> pregnant?"

She asks without hesitation. I burst into tears. I put my hands
over my eyes. I don't want to answer that question. She doesn't
touch me or try to calm me down.

She patiently waits for me to calm down on my own. I cry for a few minutes. She gently takes my hands down.

> "Baby, does anyone know you're pregnant? Even more importantly, does anyone know you are here?"

I shake my head no.

> "No one knows I'm here."

> "What are you going to do? How far along are you?"

Auntie asks. I hunch my shoulders.

> "I'm not really sure how far along I am."

> "Look, I need you to talk to me. How can I help you if you won't talk? Why did you want to come here?"

She sounds a little annoyed.

> "Because I thought you would understand what I'm going through."

I tell her softly.

> "What in heaven makes you think I will understand you coming here without permission from your aunt and uncle, PREGNANT?"

Auntie Noonie doesn't sound annoyed anymore. I love her so much, but I know she's disappointed in me.

> "I didn't know where else to go, Auntie.
> I want to keep my baby."

> "Okay, have you made a plan?"

She looks me in the eye.

> "Yes."

> "What is it?

Auntie asks. I can't speak. The baby is moving a lot. I don't know what to tell her. I put my hand on what now looks like a full-blown pregnancy belly. I hold my breath the moment I feel the baby move.

> "Love, I can't help you if you
> don't tell me what's going on?"

Her care and concern for me is overwhelming.

> "You trust me, don't you?"

> "Yes, I trust you Auntie, that's
> why I'm here."

I pause for a moment.

> "My plan is to have the baby. Finish
> school and go to college."

"Okay, first, have you told your
auntie and uncle?"

"Auntie, I can't tell them. I just can't."

I start to cry again.

"Stop crying. You didn't cry your
way into this situation and you
certainly can't cry your way out?"

"Who is the father? Does he know?
What are his wishes?"

She continues to fire question after question.

"The father is my boyfriend, Malik.
He doesn't know. I don't want him
to know. I haven't been to the doctor
yet, but I've been using this app
that tells me what to do."

"Wait, your boyfriend is the father;
and you don't want him to know?
Why not? He's the father. He needs
to know. No doctor? Come on, this
is so important, niece. What do you
know about having a baby?"

I stand up and walk to the window. I don't want her to see me
crying. I hug my arms across my body tightly. I feel protection
from within. I don't want to talk.

"Love, the father of your child needs
to know. You need to make a doctor's
appointment to see how everything is
with the baby. I see you're showing."

Her questions keep coming.

"Auntie, I google stuff and buy vitamins.
I use another app that helps me keep up
with how far along I am. I am almost
five months now."

"Rachel hasn't figured anything out?"

"No, I stay in my room. I wear baggy
sweats and hoodies."

I walk back to the table and wipe my face. Auntie Noonie's
phone rings.

"Hello," she says.

I hear the "Wicked Witch of the Ghetto talking.

"Noonie, I'm looking for Jazmyn.
I know she can't be up there, but
I'm worried about her. The school
called, they said she didn't show
up for her classes. I keep checking
with them, but they keep saying
she's not there."

"Rachel honey calm down."

She tells her and leaves the room. I can hear Auntie Rachel
yelling through the phone.

> "How can you tell me to calm down?
> That child could have been kidnapped
> or something!"

> "Rachel calm down! She's here."

I can't hear anything else, so I tried to act like I was busy
pondering our discussion. Auntie Noonie comes back in
the kitchen and says, "Rachel she's here!" Wow! She
told her upon hearing that, I just wanted to disappear.
I can only hear one side of the conversation now.

> "Yes, I picked her up from the
> airport this morning assuming
> you knew she was coming.
> I'm sorry I never checked with
> you."

Auntie Noonie says.

> "Now Rachel let's think rationally
> about this. Why don't you talk to
> her? We have to keep the lines of
> communication open with these
> kids. She's right here, talk to her."

Auntie Noonie covers the receiver and says to me,

> "Look Jazmyn, just talk to her. She's upset
> and worried, but you have to tell her
> you're pregnant. I'm not doing it for you.
> It's your responsibility."

I stand in front of her frozen. I don't want to talk to her, but I must.

"Hello?"

"Jazmyn! What are you doing out there with my sister?"

I'm silent.

"Jazmyn Jackson you hear me talking to you! You better answer me!"

I hear Uncle Benny in the background saying something and he takes the phone.

"Jazmyn, Punkin."

I start to cry at the sound of that gentle voice.

"Yes."

"Punkin, what's going on? You had us worried. The school called and said you didn't show up for classes. We even tried to call you, but you didn't answer.

"I'm sorry Uncle Benny."

I say through my crying.

"It's okay. Just tell me what's wrong.

Why have you run away? Is it that
bad here?"

"I'm sorry I disappointed you
Uncle Benny."

"How did you disappoint me, Punkin?"

I take a moment. I have to tell him.

"Uncle Benny, I'm pregnant."

There's a pause.

"You're pregnant? Okay you could
have come to me. I can help you."

I can hear Auntie Rachel screaming in the background.

"PREGNANT! I told you Benny
she was nothing but trouble. I'm
worrying about her and SHE'S
PREGNANT! That little tramp."

"Rachel please let me talk to
the girl."

Uncle Benny snaps.

"I didn't know what to say and I
thought you would be mad at me."

"Punkin I've always told you that
you could tell me anything, no
matter how bad it is."

Uncle Benny pleads.

"I'm not upset. We just have to
figure out things moving
forward. Okay?"

Evil Auntie Rachel shouting.

"Figure what out! I'm figuring
nothing out. What I do know is
she can't come back here.
Benny, I don't want her back
here!"

"Rachel! Stop! Where is she going
to live? Let me talk to her! Please!"

I've never heard him raise his voice like that and I didn't hear
her anymore either.

"I always knew she hated me."

"She doesn't hate you. Don't worry
about anything. Just let me talk to
her. We will talk to Noonie and
figure things out. For now, you
need to see a doctor and stay
focused on your baby. I love you
Punkin."

"I love you too Uncle Benny. Bye.

I hang up, and call for Auntie Noonie.

"Auntie!"

"Yes, baby girl. What did he say?"

"He just said you guys will figure
something out. Auntie Rachel
hates me though. She was yelling
like crazy. I've never heard
Uncle Benny yell at her like that.
I'm tired now. Do you mind if I
go and take a nap? I'm very sleepy."

"Well, this isn't a small issue sweetheart.
We will figure it out, but that includes
you coming up with some of your own
solutions. Yes, you can take a nap. We
can talk when you wake up. Go get
some rest. Your baby needs it."

I walk to my room and lay on the fluffy white comforter. My body sinks into the mattress. My head becomes one with the soft feathery pillows. I am catapulted into a deep afternoon nap.

Chapter Six

Since I told Uncle Benny, I wonder what he and Auntie Witch are talking about. He's probably sitting in his big chair relaxing and watching re-runs of old movies.

"Benny, I told you that girl would be nothing but trouble. When we picked her up from the hospital, I could see it."

"Rachel stop. Let's be real here. You never liked my family. The only reason you went along with Jazmyn coming here is because I wouldn't have it any other way. She has no one else! I will always be there for her. I'm fine if you don't want to be involved. Just remember, you're my wife and we took vows before God. Now part of those vows meant through thick and thin."

"Yeah, and it's been thick since she got here. God doesn't expect me to be a fool. I can clearly see this is foolishness."

"Rachel, Jazmyn is pregnant now."

"And at my sister's house, my family.
Not yours. Where are they?"

"Well obviously she felt comfortable enough
to confide in her. She could have turned to
one of her friends. Thank God she has
Noonie to talk to."

Uncle Benny says. Auntie Rachel sits swinging her crossed
leg back and forth rapidly with her arms tight across her body.

"What do you have against my
family, Rachel?"

"Benjamin! I don't have anything
against your family."

Rachel stated firmly.

"Okay, then why do you hate our
little girl so much."

"She's not OUR LITTLE girl. She's
your niece and I don't hate her. I just
think she causes problems in our
household."

Benny takes a deep breath and rubs his forehead.

"Problems? What problems? Tell me
what do you have against her? She
gets her chores done.

Her grades are impeccable. Jazmyn never
talks back like I hear the other kids. You
are always on her, fussing about the dishes.
She washes the dishes. You fuss about her
clothes. Rachel, you made a chore chart
and penned rules. You fuss at her for
following the rules and you fuss at her for
not following the rules. She doesn't know
when she's doing right or wrong. I stay
out of that, so she gets to know how to be
a lady from you and respect your rules.
What's the real problem?"

Rachel leaves the kitchen abruptly. She calls her sister Noonie.
Rachel says,

"Hey Girl. Be careful with that Lil Huzzy
you have in your house."

Noonie says.

"Whoa, whoa, whoa, that's uncalled
for Rachel. She made a mistake
and needs help."

I hear her walk into her room and close the door. I was too
tired to hear the rest. So, I fall fast asleep. Minutes later I
hear,

"Hey, sleepyhead. It's time to get
up. How did you sleep?"

"It was okay. I still feel tired."

"Well, you need to shower and
change your clothes. We have
a doctor's appointment. There
isn't much time. The clinic
closes at seven and your appt
is at six."

"Where? I don't really want to go
to the doctor. I thought we were
going tomorrow."

"Look, you have about thirty
minutes to get dressed. I will
see you downstairs, young
lady. Get ready to go."

She speaks with supreme authority. I really think that I should
take a shower. I move fast too. When I get downstairs, she is
just wrapping a sandwich in a napkin on the counter for me.
I'm glad because I'm starving.

"Get that sandwich, bag of chips,
the water, and let's get out of here.
I want you to be on time so we can
get the information we need about
this baby."

My phone is off, so I don't know how many people have been
calling me. I turn it on, and it keeps making noise for the
messages. Ding, Ding, Ding!! It makes noise for a very long
time, but I don't want to look at it.

"My goodness, girl! When was
the last time you looked at your
phone?"

"When I got off the plane."

"How did you get to the airport
Jazz?"

Now she's being nosey.

"My friend, Sean got me a car
that took me to the airport."

I paused and I think to myself, I'm getting a little irritated with
all these questions. Then she questions me again.

"Who is that? It doesn't sound
like it's your boyfriend."

I can tell she wants to know more, but I'm not going to force
anything. I only answer the questions she asks. Adults set you
up by asking questions and then using the information against
you later.

"He's just a friend I met,"

I answer looking out of the window. I'm praying the questions
will stop. I pull my phone out to check my text messages.

"Wait, wait, wait where is the father?
Who is he again?"

She interrupts with more questions.

> "He's around. His name is Malik,
> remember?"

> "Why don't you want to tell him?"

> "Because."

Because! "You do know that 'Because'
is not an answer, don't you?"

I feel like I'm being interrogated. This seatbelt is too tight
across my body and is getting uncomfortable. I start to tug at
it to get it loose from across my belly. Besides that, I'm very
irritated by her line of questioning.

> "Why aren't you telling Malik?
> He's your boyfriend, right?"

She is firm and wants answers.

> "Yeah, he is.

Right on que Malik sends a text to my phone.

> *Malik - Jazzy you better text or call me*
> *back. I want to talk to you.*
> *You can't break up with me.*
> *Malik - Jazz*
> *Malik - Jazzy where did you go?*
> *Malik - When are you coming back?*
> *Malik - Big Mama said you looked pregnant.*
> *Are you hiding cuz you pregnant?*
> *Malik - Are we having a baby Jazz?*

*Malik- If you don't call or text me, I'm gonna
find you and you won't like it.*

His text is all over the place. I decided to answer.

Me - Please leave me alone Malik.

I get very quiet in the car. Thankfully, we pull into the clinic
parking lot. We get out of the car. There is still silence between
us. As we walk to the main entrance, the gravel is crunching
under my feet. My little munchkin starts moving around a lot.
I'm so nervous. My heart is beating fast. It feels like the baby
is literally banging on my chest trying to jump out. Auntie
opens the door to the clinic. When we walk in, I look around
at the people. There are a lot of people here, and it seems like
they are all staring at me. This clinic is nothing like I thought.
It's clean and smells like Tropical Breeze air freshener. There
are small blue couches that two people can share. A small
generic brown table rests in front of them. All televisions
display women's health information. The waiting room isn't
very big, but it's okay because there are only five pregnant
women waiting to be seen. Of course, these women are all
grown. I feel a lady gazing upon me. She looks me up and
down, down and up with sheer disgust. The other ladies in
here are minding their own business reading magazines
or tending to their children. I was so busy looking around
while walking, I had not realized Auntie Noonie had stopped.
I bump right into her back at the check in window. We look
like "The Three Stooges" minus one.

"MAY I HELP YOU?"

The lady behind the counter yells. I am immediately
embarrassed. Auntie is very quiet and proper.

"Yes, we are here for an appointment
for Jazmyn Jackson."

"JAZZZZZMMYYYNNN JACKSON!
WHAT'S HER DATE OF BIRTH
MA'AM?"

She yells. I wonder if she's hard of hearing or trying to
embarrass me.

"Jazz, get up here and talk to
this woman."

Auntie turns to me. I think she's annoyed at the yelling too.

I whisper, "November 11th."

"I'M SORRY, NOVEMBER
WHAT? AND I NEED THE
YEAR TOO PLEASE?"

The lady continues to yell. I whisper again.

"Uhhhhhmmm, November 11, 2006."

I turn to see if anyone is looking, but everyone is doing
something else or at least pretending to.

"JAZZZZZMMYYYNNNN,
YOU'RE SIXTEEN!"

She yells. I'm convinced this lady is trying to embarrass me. I
get mad. Just before I begin to say something to her, she hands
me a clipboard to fill papers out.

"Auntie, why she gotta be so loud?"

I whisper to her.

> "Honey, she wasn't loud. Maybe
> you just thought she was loud
> because you are a little
> embarrassed."

She says. I roll my eyes and start to work on the stack of papers given to me. Most of it is easy until it asks about my parent's medical history. I have no idea if my parents had anything or not. No one talks to me about health issues. Does high blood pressure, diabetes, headaches or anything else run in my family? This is my frustration.

> "Auntie, I don't know anything
> about my parents' medical
> background."

I say sadly.

> "Okay, you have to skip it. You can't
> make it up. Keep going before they
> call you into the room. By the way,
> I will be coming into the room with
> you."

Auntie directs. I don't really care if she comes in the room with me or not. I prefer that she comes in. I'm getting scared. I don't know what they do once they close the door behind you. Just as I begin to sign my name, I look up to see a big curvy black woman come out.

> "Jazmym Jackson."

Auntie Noonie and I stand simultaneously and walk through the door.

> "Hi, Jazmyn. My name is Laneka.
> I'm your nurse."

She stops once we get inside the back area. We look at her and wonder why we are stopping. Then Laneka leads us to one of the cold exam rooms. It's cold, but nice also. The chair in the room is plush and soft. Auntie sits in that one. It's a matching blue like the couches in the waiting area. The exam table is the usual ugly beige pleather cushion with tissue paper laid on top.

> "Jazmyn, you don't have to have
> your mom in the room if you
> don't want to. You can have
> privacy if you want."

> "She will be fine with me in the room.
> Thank you for your concern."

Auntie responds. While still in the room, Laneka begins to type information onto the computer. She takes my blood pressure. She has me step on a scale.

> "Ok Jazmyn, you weigh
> one hundred and ten pounds."

After gathering all the information, we enter another exam
room. Laneka gives me instructions, asks me to remove my
clothes and hands me a gown. Seconds later she states,

> "Jazmyn, I understand your mom
> will be in the room, are you fine
> with that?"

She gives Auntie the death stare. Auntie stares deep into her
eyes as if she was waiting for an argument. I thought they
were about to have a fight in the exam room.

> "Yes, I want her in here."

> "Okay, the doctor will be here
> in a moment."

She says and walks out the door. Auntie seems irritated, but I
dare not to question her. I'm very nervous. Terrified because I
haven't any idea what is going to happen. Well, at least I will
find out how far along I really am. I feel like the app is on
point and my calculations are accurate. I am laying on my
back when this cute little lady comes in. She is a short little
petite black lady. She introduces herself as Dr. Smith. Auntie
sits quietly in the room. She is so unassuming, I forgot that she
was in here. I want her to ask questions or say something.
Nevertheless, she sits there in the corner like the thinker
statue, sculpted by Auguste Rodin.

> "So, Miss Jazmyn, did you give a
> urine sample?"

The Doctor asks as she flips through pages on the clipboard.

"Ummm, no."

I hate sounding like I'm scared. The fact is I am terrified! She reaches over and she hands me a cup and says,

"Urinate in the cup and bring it back."

The cup was little; and I am not sure how to do it.

"Read the instructions, put the cup
under your stream of urine and
get a little in there. You don't need
a lot. You can relieve yourself of
the rest in the toilet. Wash your
hands and I will meet you right here."

She leaves the room. I am so confused. How am I supposed to get pee in this little bitty cup. I go to the bathroom. I begin to perform the task and I feel warm urine flowing all over my hand. A sick feeling comes over me as the pee runs through my fingers down to my wrist. It's all in there. I say to myself. I wipe the cup down, wash my hands, and come out to a room filled with laughter. The doctor and Auntie are laughing as if they are old friends.

"Okay, Jazmyn hop back on the
table so we can get a look. Did
you take a pregnancy test prior
to your appointment?

Dr. Smith says.

"Clearly you are pregnant."

"Yes, I took two tests," I mumble.

"Excuse me, doctor."

Auntie interrupts.

"Look, Jazmyn, you are going
to have to speak up and talk to
this doctor. She needs to hear
you."

She blows out air from her mouth in frustration and rolls her
eyes. I don't understand why.

"It's okay, I can hear her. This is a
big thing for a sixteen year old."

Dr. Smith speaks with understanding and compassion in her
voice, unlike Auntie.

"With the two tests you took, they
were both positive?"

"Yes."

"Okay, I'm going to raise your gown
up past your stomach and I'm going to
put a cold slimy gel on your belly.
I will do an ultrasound to see this baby.
It will help to see how far along you
are. Have you seen a doctor?
Or do you have any idea how far
along you are?"

She asks, while looking at her computer.

"No, I haven't seen a doctor.I have
apps that I use to help me figure
stuff out. I think I'm about five
months. I've been taking my
prenatal vitamins since I found out.
I try to eat some good food too. I
was sick in the beginning. I learned
that I have to eat so I'm not nauseous."

"Okay."

She turns and looks at the clipboard.

"You weigh one hundred and ten
pounds; you're pretty petite. Let
me look at the baby.

Dr. Smith squeezes the jelly junk on my belly and puts the
thing with the cord attached to it on my belly.

It's cold!

"Okay, let's see what we have
here, Miss Jazmyn."

Pointing at the screen, Dr. Smith says,

"See this little thing moving like
a flicker?"

"Yes."

I look over at the screen.

"That's your baby's heartbeat.

We will listen to it when I'm
done with this part. But here is
the head and his arms and legs.
Can you see that?"

Dr. Smith moves the thing on the cord around my belly and
didn't say much. Once she finished, she wipes the goop off
my belly and picks up something else. She shows it to me and
explains that we can hear my baby's heartbeat. As I listen, a
big smile grows upon my face. I am so shocked. My baby's
heart is beating so fast. There's a person with a heartbeat
inside me.

"That's your baby's heartbeat, mom."

Dr. Smith says with a smile.

"Wow. So fast."

I am amazed.

"Yes, they are fast like that when they
are in mommy's belly and when they
come out."

"Okay."

"The heartbeat is strong and sounds
really good. Let me measure your
belly and I will tell you how far along
you are. Looks like we've got a healthy
baby boy in there."

Dr. Smith states. She pulls out a measuring tape and puts it from the top of my belly to the bottom. She writes something on her clipboard.

> "Okay, mom, you are seven and a half months along. Your due date is March 1st."

> "Did you say a boy?"

> "Yes, I did. Little lady, you are having a boy," she says with a smile.

I don't smile. I just look at the ceiling in shock. What will I do with a little boy? I thought I was having a girl. I wanted a girl. I don't want a boy like Malik. What if he turns into an abuser like his father? What if he gets a young girl pregnant? What am I going to do?

> "Jazmyn, Jazmyn, are you okay?"

I can hear the doctor calling my name. My mind is in another zone.

> "Yeah, I'm fine."

I say as I sit up.

> "Okay, so this is what I want you to do. You need to make an appointment with your primary physician as soon as possible. You need to get caught up with everything because you are going into your third trimester. It's important that you see a doctor regularly from this point forward.

"Okay."

I answer.

"Do you have any questions for
me?"

Dr. Smith asks.

"No."

I say looking at the ground. I'm stunned as if I just found
out I'm pregnant.

"Noonie, any questions for me?"

Dr. Smith asks Auntie.

"Yes, I don't know if you said it
or not, but is her weight okay?
Since she's always so petite,
I'm wondering if she is gaining
enough weight."

Auntie Noonie asks

"Jazmyn, did you weigh yourself
when you first got pregnant?"

Dr. Smith asks.

"Ummmm, no, but I weighed about
ninety-four pounds the last time
I got on the scale."

"Okay, you are one ten now. You need to gain at least ten more pounds. I don't want you gaining too much weight because if the baby is too big for your little frame, you may have to have a C-section."

Dr. Smith pauses.

"Any more questions?"

"What's a C-section? I mean. I know what it is, but can you tell me how it would be if I had one."

"It is a major surgery. We numb you from the waist down, cut your lower abdomen, and take the baby out that way. You don't feel much, but if you can't deliver naturally that's what will happen. That's why you have to find a doctor as soon as possible."

"Okay, so if the baby is too big, I will have to do that?"

"Yes, because you are a very petite young lady. Now on the flip side, if you don't gain enough weight, the baby can have complications. Make sure you are eating the allotted calories that's in the notebook my nurse gives you. Also, read all of the literature. It will have information you need to prepare for childbirth."

"Okay."

I am laying on the table taking in all this information. The cutting me open terrifies me and can't even imagine them taking my baby out that way. I can't even imagine my baby coming out the way it's supposed to.

"Okay, if you don't have any more questions, get dressed and I will have the nurse give you the summary of your visit and your notebook."

I start feeling sick when the door closes. I lay back on the table for a minute.

"What's wrong? Too much information?"

"I feel sick."

I put one hand on my bulging seven and a half month bump and one over my mouth. Auntie Noonie grabs the trash can and stands next to the bed. I sit up quickly and vomit in the trash can. I haven't been sick in a month. I thought this was over.

"Lay there until you feel better."

She gets a paper towel, wets it, gives it to me to wipe my face and mouth in an effort to help me feel better. It works a little, but I still feel the nausea. Someone knocks on the door.

"Hiiiiiii, it's Laneka again. Here is your summary and information notebook. Make sure you go to a regular doctor to get your care as soon as possible. Doctor Smith says, if you can't find one, give her a call. She can help you."

"Thank you,"

I say as I take the paper with the notebook and hand it to Auntie Noonie.

"Why are you handing that to me? I'm not pregnant."

She didn't even raise her hand to take it. While holding the paper in my hand, I slide off the table to get dressed. When we get in the car, Auntie Noonie is quiet. I begin to get a little nervous. My phone starts vibrating. I don't want to look at it. When I finally look at my phone, I have a lot of missed calls. Eight calls are from Malik. I had no idea what I was going to say. There were also texts from Mimi, Sean, and one of my teachers. I didn't want to talk to anyone. My mind is so clouded with everything I just experienced. Auntie Noonie interrupts my thoughts.

"Okay, I need to hear a solid plan on what you are planning to do. You are due in a few months. What about the father? Will he be involved? Are you going to tell him? Do you have a ticket to go back home?"

Auntie Noonie fires questions. I put my phone in my lap. Look out of the window and I feel warm tears roll down my face. I quickly swipe them from my cheeks. I just can't believe I am pregnant and dealing with a stupid boy for a father. I know I can do it, but being a mom at sixteen isn't in my plans. I final ly look at my phone and I read only Malik's messages.

> *Malik -*   *Jazzy where are you?*
> *Malik -*   *You better answer me.*
> *Malik –*   *Jazzy, I love you and*
>   *I wanna make things*
>   *right.*
> *Malik -*   *I wanna be a father*
>   *to our kid.*

How does he know I'm pregnant? How could he have found that out?

> *Jazzy -*   *Malik leave me alone. I don't want*
>   *anything to do with you. There*
>   *is no baby.*

Malik immediately responds.

> *Malik -*   *Jazzy! Please I wanna see you*
>   *I know you left town. You*
>   *looked dead at me when*
>   *I passed you at the airport.*
>   *I will find you and MY BABY.*
> *Jazzy -*   *LEAVE ME ALONE*

"Do you hear me talking to you?"

Auntie Noonie interrupts my thoughts.

> "Of course, I hear you. I'm in the
> car with you."

I say as I wipe my tears away.

> "Look, don't you dare get smart
> with me. I'm trying to help you.
> What I don't need from you is a
> smart remark like that. You think
> about what I asked you; and I
> expect answers by the time we
> start eating dinner."

She is done with the conversation. Auntie Noonie waits for a few minutes. Then, Auntie Noonie speaks again.

> "What are your plans?"

> "Auntie, I don't know. I don't know.
> I – don't knooooowwww."

I start to cry. It's too much pressure. I'm thinking about everything. I thought about some of these things but not like this. She didn't say anything as I begin to sob.

> "Look, Jazz. I want to help you, but I can't help you if I don't know where your head is. I need to know what your plans are."

We pull into her garage, I gather my things, and we walk into the house without a word. Auntie starts dinner. I lay on the bed, bury my head in my pillow and cry as hard as I can. My stomach is feeling queasy. When I come up for air, I'm sweating. My face is red. My eyes are puffy and my hair is a mess. I have no idea how long I had been there, but Auntie Noonie busts through the door and tells me to come eat dinner. It smells so good. Nice distraction.

Chapter Seven

There's a peaceful silence at the dinner table. All you can hear is a fork scraping a plate. Oftentimes, you hear the sound of our cups being placed on the table. I know it's coming. Eventually she'll ask me a question. Uh oh. Here it comes. She sits her knife and fork down on her plate. She wipes her mouth and asks,

> "Have you thought about what I asked you earlier?"

She looks at me. I look down.

> "Yes."

> "And?"

> "Which part did you want to know?"

I ask knowing it's a stupid question.

> "Don't play with me! What are your plans?"

> "Stay here.

> "Stay here? Stay here and do what?"

Auntie Noonie chuckles.

"Stay here, live and raise my baby. I will go to school. There are schools that have daycares in them, and some also have buses that come to get you. If the bus won't come and get me I will take public transportation to school. You won't have to worry about me. I will take care of me and the baby."

"Jazzy, I don't know about that, sweetie. You and a baby here. My life isn't set up like that. I am a single woman. I have no children for a reason. I'm retired and responsible only for me. I'm not sure that will work, honey."

"Please don't make me go back to Auntie Rachel, she's going to kick me out on the streets."

I beg her.

"I don't have anywhere to go."

"What makes you think she's going to kick you out?"

Auntie Noonie says and looks at me like I am sounding ridiculous.

"She really didn't want me there in the first place. I always heard her talking to Uncle B when I first moved there, and she kept asking him why they had to keep me? Why couldn't I go somewhere else? There wasn't anyone else to go to. Uncle B said he wasn't having anyone else raise me. They didn't know I could hear them. You heard her on the phone. She was yelling that I can't come back. Technically, I'm already kicked out. Uncle B is the only one that cares about me. She just fusses at me and never says anything nice. I try to stay out of her way as much as possible, but that's hard sometimes. I try to do everything she tells me to, but that's never enough. So, I know she doesn't like me,"

Auntie Noonie replies,

"I don't think that's true. How did you keep the pregnancy from her this long? I noticed when you were here for Christmas. Your face was fuller, and you wouldn't look me in the eye. You also stayed sleep more than normal. I didn't want to say anything when you were here because I didn't want to cause any problems. I know how my sister can be."

"You could tell? I thought I kept it hidden
pretty good. I am surprised someone
knew. Auntie Rachel doesn't pay attention
to me like that. So, I always wear baggy
clothes. Uncle B asked a few questions,
but I answer him with something quick
and keep talking. It often distracted
him from what he initially asked."

I get up and begin to clear the table so I can wash dishes.
Looks like that evil woman taught me something. Auntie
Noonie watches me without saying a word. Clearly the line of
questioning is over for the evening.

I have now been here for a few weeks. I'm in school taking
classes online. It's a school for pregnant teens. They prefer we
attend online to make it easier on us. I do attend one class on
campus every Wednesday, but that's okay the class is great.
It's an early morning parenting class. It's very interesting and
filled with valuable information. The type of information that
every mom should know, not just a single teen mom. The
instructor, Mrs. Presley, is very engaging and personal. She
tells us, "I know what you are going through. I've been there.
You can get through it. We will navigate through this
together." I really enjoy her teaching style. She makes my
other classes seem useless. I'm doing exceptionally well in all
of them though. In fact, the last time I checked my grades,
they were all A's and they should be. All I do is study, read my
bible, read parenting books, self help books and talk to Auntie
Noonie. My Auntie Noonie is really organized and is teaching
me to be the same way. A few days after I moved here, she
purchased me a calendar and books. I did say that I read and
study, right?

Our discussions were very scary in the beginning. I always tried to avoid them, but now I look forward to conversing with her. Our bible studies are second to none. She gives me scriptures to read every night and we talk about them. She wants me to memorize them, but that's a lot right now. When she first gave me the Bible, she had a long, long, long, talk with me.

"Jazmyn do you know the Lord?"

Auntie Noonie said.

"Yes I do."

"Do you pray regularly and did you go to church with your aunt and uncle?"

"I don't really pray. I used to with my mom and dad. We went to church every Sunday, but when I went to live with them we hardly went. Then Auntie started going by herself, leaving us behind."

"Now is the time to start getting to know Jesus and learning more about Him. You want to build your relationship with Him. Have you accepted Him as your personal savior?"

Auntie asks.

"Yes, I did with Uncle Benny, but nobody told me what to do after that."

"Okay, I will help you with that because
you want to be in prayer about everything,
but you also have to incorporate reading
the bible. This road that you have
chosen as a single mother isn't going to
be easy, and you will need the Lord to
help you down or on that path."

"Thanks Auntie Noonie, I want to
learn to pray so I can teach my little
man how to pray."

She says,

"That's very good. Now listen and
remember this, Jazzy. You must feed
your spirit as well as your body.
Never forget that."

Feeding my spirit is something new that I had to learn. I also
had to learn to feed my body correctly too. I didn't realize
that Hot Cheetos, Takis, and McDonalds are considered junk
food. Well, they are in her eyes. She doesn't allow me to eat
like I used to. No junk food. Every once in a while, I can
have a sweet treat, but no Hot Cheetos or Takis. I plan to have
a big bag of Takis after I have my baby. I miss my spicy foods
so much. The only thing I crave that's healthy is a cucumber. I
love cucumbers. I can eat them all day long. I don't have to
put anything on them either. I can either cut them up or eat
them whole like a pickle. Eating healthy is going to take some
time. If I had my way, junk food would be the most important
part of my diet. Sadly, Auntie Noonie and Dr. Smith would
hunt me down like hound dogs to take my Takis. I can hear
them now. "Jazmyn, you're eating for two now. If you want a
healthy baby you must eat right."

I know it's for my own good and the baby's health. You know, I really feel blessed to have two voices of reason guiding my maternal path. The pregnancy hasn't been easy. That's why I choose to stick with Dr. Smith because I really like her. I am very comfortable with her. Turns out Dr. Smith and Auntie Noonie are friends. I knew something was up with them. I like her anyway. She talks to me like a real person. Everyone else talks around me like I'm not there. She understands that I am the one who is pregnant. I'm confident she will do a great job in bringing my baby into this world. Unfortunately, Malik will not be a positive male role model in his life. I really hope my Uncle Benny becomes a major influence in his life.

Speaking of Uncle Benny. I miss my uncle. He tries to call me all the time to check up on me. I always tell him, with Dr. Smith, Auntie Noonie and Jesus I'm in good hands. My true concern is Uncle Benny. He doesn't sound the same when I talk to him. His speech is slower. He's wheezing and doesn't appear to be as energetic over the phone as before I left. I could be reading more into it, but I'm concerned about his health. It can be really difficult to live a happy and healthy life with the evil witch he's married to. Keep in mind, that I'm leaving out the B for spiritual reasons. I feel bad for him because he tells me how much he misses me and loves me. I love him too. One thing confuses me though. Why hasn't he or "The Wicked Witch of the West" asked me who is the father of my baby. Only Auntie Noonie asked that question. Uh oh, I can smell breakfast. I can smell nauseating bacon. I don't want to go downstairs. I'm very tired and not very hungry. Doctor Smith wants me to eat more food. She says I need to gain at least five pounds by my next visit on Monday. I just don't feel like eating though.

"Jazmyn! Come down here and
eat, girl!"

She yells from downstairs.

"I'm coming, Auntie,"

I finally get up, put on some sweats, a big t-shirt, and some
fuzzy socks. I waddle downstairs.

"Were you sleeping again?"

She asks. I yawn with my mouth wide open.

"Yeah, I can't stay awake. I'm so tired."

"You okay? You look kind of pale."

"The smell of bacon. It's making me
nauseous."

She places a plate in front of me. I think to myself. This is a
lot of food. I can't eat all of this. I take a deep breath and try to
eat the food. My phone sounds with a text message.

Unknown - Hey Jazzy, where you at?
Jazz- Who dis?
Unknown - A very good friend of yours.
       We haven't spoken in a while.
       Remember me? Lorenzo?
Jazzy - Oh yes how are you?

I never saved Lorenzo's number in my phone.

> *Unknown - I'm cool. Where you been I*
> *haven't seen you at school*
> *for a while.*
>
> *Jazzy - Oh my aunt wanted me to*
> *homeschool so I'm stayin*
> *home for the rest of the school*
> *year.*
>
> *Unknown - So, can I come by and visit?*
> *I wanna hang out and just see*
> *how you doin?*
>
> *Jazzy - Well my people don't want me*
> *to have any company right*
> *now. I don't know why. Maybe*
> *another time.*
>
> *Unknown - You still stay on Eucalyptus,*
> *right?*
>
> *Jazzy - Yeah.*

I start to feel a little weird about this conversation. Lorenzo knows where I live because we use to walk home from school daily before we started high school.

> *Unknown - I think I remember where*
> *the house is. Let me know*
> *when you can have company*
> *again. Did you get in trouble*
> *or something?*
>
> *Jazzy - No, my people just wanted me*
> *to try homeschooling to see*
> *if I could advance even more*
> *and graduate a year early.*
> *How are things going at school*
> *for you?*
>
> *Unknown - It's cool.*

> *Jazzy - Okay I gotta go. Nice talking to you.*
> *Unknown - So when can I come through?*

I'm not going to tell him where I am. I just really don't think it's Lorenzo. This is so weird.

> *Jazzy - I will let you know, right now is*
> *not a good time.*
> *Unknown - Cool, I will check with you later.*

I immediately call Mimi. She might have Lorenzo's number. I want to see if that was really him.

> "Mimi, do you have Lorenzo's
> number? I need it."

> "Girl what's going on? Why do you
> sound like this?"

I can tell that Mimi is scrolling through her phone.

> "I just finished texting someone that said
> they were Lorenzo. It didn't seem like
> that was him. I think it was Malik."

> "You can't just call him and ask if he
> text you. What will you say if he says
> yes?"

> "I will just say it didn't seem like it was
> him. He wanted to come over and all
> that. Lorenzo has never asked
> to come to my house. It was just a
> weird texting thing. I'm suspicious."

"How about I call on the three-way?
You mute your phone and just listen."

I will see if he has talked to you lately."

"Great idea! That's why you're my best
friend!"

Mimi calls him. The phone rings six times before he answers.

"What up Mimi?"

"Hey Zo, Whatchu doin'?"

"Nothin' just chillin' at the crib."

"Have you seen or heard from Jazz lately?"

"Naahh! I haven't seen her in a minute.
We were cool back in the day. Ever
since she hooked up with that buster,
she ain't got no love for me. Why?
What up?"

"I haven't seen her myself."

"What? Not choo. She put the chill on
you? Wow, I don't feel so bad now."

"Yeah, she's still my girl though."

"Yeah, true that. That's real talk."

"Alright, Zo. Let me track her down."

"Yeah, do that. Late."

They hang up.

"So, he didn't text me. I bet that was
Malik. I don't want him to find me!"

"Wait girl don't panic. He can't find
you in Northern California."

I tell her, "You don't know that!"

"Girl, what is up with you? I thought you
were just going to the Bay to think
about things. You're in school and all
that out there."

Mimi changes the subject.

"Mimi, Malik is very abusive."

"Abusive how? No way."

"You won't believe all the things
he's done to me."

"Like what Jazzy? Yell at you?
Danny gets mad and yells at
me sometimes."

"He yells and he's physical. He
pushed me down where I've hit
my head. He's grabbed and left
bruises. He always apologizes.
Well, most of the time.

I'm scared of him. I'm afraid he's going
to hurt me or even worse, our son."

There is silence.

"Hello?"

"I'm here.".

I hear her sniff and take a deep breath. I know she's crying.
That made me feel bad.

"Jazz, I am so sorry. Why didn't you tell
me before? When I saw those bruises on
your arm, that was Malik huh? Have
you at least told your aunt up there?"
"Maybe you should talk to her about
that. If he happens to come and find you,
she won't be surprised at how he might
act. She can be ready to call the police."

"I need to think about that."

"She might be able to help. Hey, I have
to go my mom's calling me."

"Okay text me later then, Bye."

I finally get in the shower. It feels so good. I made it super hot.
I like to let the water run on my body for a while. I always
wash my hair too. The prenatal pills that I take made my hair
grow so long and thick.

Auntie knocks on the bathroom door.

> "Hey, hurry up! Your thirty minutes
> are up. I want to beat the crowd."

> "Auntie Noonie, crowd? What crowd?
> You keep saying hurry up before the
> crowd."

> "First of all, I don't like going to the store
> when everyone is there shopping, THAT
> CROWD! Next you need to stop wearing
> all of those tight sweats, they are too small.
> You should have maternity clothes. They
> are made to accommodate a growing belly.
> You look ridiculous with your belly showing."

> "Well, I don't like maternity clothes,
> they're ugly."

> "Well guess what? It ain't what you like.
> I bet you don't like being pregnant
> either, but you are. So, you are getting
> maternity clothes and you are wearing
> them. You have money in your account
> and clothing is allotted in your budget.
> I'm sure you saw that."

Auntie Noonie explains through the bathroom door.

> "I saw it, but I wasn't budgeting for
> maternity clothes. I was saving for
> the next pair of Jordans coming out
> next month."

"Jordans! Jordans! You are having
a baby and your days of the latest
Jordans are over."

She says, with a chuckle.

"Now get out of this bathroom."

"Okay! I just have to rinse the
soap from my hair!"

I decide to move faster so I can be ready to go. I rush to get
out of the shower and slip on the floor. I scream while still on
the floor. I'm scared and immediately start crying. Auntie is
knocking on the door.

"Jazmyn, are you okay? Jazmyn?
Can you open the door baby?"

"No, Auntie, help me!" I cry.
I'm afraid to move.

She unlocks the door. I'm on the floor leaning against the
shower door naked. My butt hurts and my belly is tight.

"Oh, my goodness, girl, what were
you doing?"

"I was just trying to get out of the
shower and slipped and fell. I
couldn't reach my towel."

"Okay, how do you feel? Does it feel
like everything is okay with the baby?"

Auntie Nonnie is so calm.

> "I don't know. My butt is hurting and
> my stomach feels tight."

> "Let's get you up and dressed. I want
> to get you checked to make sure
> everything is okay."

She helps me up. I begin to dry off, but I keep feeling the
tightness in my stomach. It keeps coming and going. Auntie is
downstairs sitting at the table ready to go. I have sweat pants
under my belly and a hoodie tightly pulled over my belly.
Everything is tight. We get in the car and she calls her friend
the doctor to see if she is available.

> "I thought you had to call the nurses
> and they made the appointments?"

I interrupt.
> "Hold on girl."

She turns to me.

> "Jazmyn if you don't stop talking to me
> while I'm on the phone you are gonna
> have more problems than being
> pregnant."

I roll my eyes. I guess I forgot who I was talking to. She
continues her phone conversation.

"Anyway, she slipped getting out of the
shower and now she's having tightness
and I just want to get her checked to
make sure she's okay."

Auntie Noonie says.

I can't hear what Dr. Smith is saying, but I assumed we are
meeting her at the office because of the direction we are going.

"Are we going to see Dr. Smith?"

I have to stop and breathe for a minute. I feel pain shoot around
my stomach.

"What's going on? Why are you
holding your breath like that?"

She is concerned now.

"I'm okay, I just feel that tightness
and it hurts this time."

I say that and feel another one.

"Well, that was only a few minutes apart.
Try to just breathe, in through your nose
and out through your mouth."

I start doing what she says and it doesn't feel as bad. We pull
into the parking lot of the hospital, not Dr. Smith's office. I
can't walk too fast because I feel pain in the bottom of my
stomach. When we get inside, the nurse is there.

Her badge reads Desiree.

> "Jazmyn come on back and take off
> all of your clothes, put the gown on
> and lay on the bed."

She says as we walk down the hall. I always smell a strong
odor of alcohol. I hate it. As we walk down the hall the pains
keep coming and going. I walk slowly hoping it will stop. I
enter the room and begin to undress. Dr. Smith comes right in
shortly thereafter.

> "So, missy you slipped getting out of
> the shower huh?"

> "Yes." I say and holding my breath
> because of the pain.

She touches my stomach. It's hard. She keeps her hand there
and looks at her watch.

> "Okay your contractions are pretty
> close together. I want you to be
> admitted. The nurse will come get
> you when it's time to move. We
> will do more once you have a
> room, but I'm a little concerned
> because your contractions are so
> close and you are feeling pain in
> your lower abdomen. You aren't
> due for another month and a half.
> Let's see if we can keep this little
> baby in there a little longer."

Dr. Smith says. I can't even talk. I'm scared, in pain and start
to cry again. I need to text Mimi.

*Jazzy - Hey girl I'm at the hospital.
I don't know what's going on
but I'm in pain and having
contractions. They are real
close together. I think they
are going to monitor me. I'm
not ready to have this baby yet.
I still have another month.*

I put my phone under my leg because they are now admitting me and rolling my bed to another room. Auntie Noonie caught me putting it under my leg and took it. She said she would hold it until I got settled in my room.

Chapter Eight

I T'S FIRST AND TEN AT MIDFIELD AND THE GAME IS
TIED!
      "Benny! Benny!

"Why do you have that so loud!" Rachel walks over and turns the sound down on the television. He doesn't realize that she turned it down.

He says,

> "Ray I miss my baby girl. Have
> you heard from her? Or your sister?"

> "Benny, that girl ain't gonna call me;
> and yes I talked to my sister."

She didn't volunteer any more information.

> "How is she doing? Did you even ask?
> The last time I talked to her she was
> good. I'm just worried about her having
> a baby and not being here. My brother
> would want me to have her here to care
> for her."

> "Well, your brother ain't here so you
> have no control over that girl."

"You really don't like her, do you?"
Since our last conversation, I've
had time to think about it.

"Now Benny, why would you ask
me that?

"You talk to her like you don't like her.
You never really took her places with
you that weren't necessary. You just
never liked her. I think she knew it too."

"Awe Benny, watch your game and stop
talking about all that foolishness. Let
me read my book in peace."

The phone rings.

"Mmmhello," He answers.

"Hey Benny this is Noonie."

"I know, I have caller ID."

He snaps.

"Okay, we don't have time for
your attitude. The doctor just
admitted Jazzy into the hospital
because she slipped getting out
of the shower."

"She fell!"

His heart starts racing as he sits up in his chair.

"Wait what? She fell. How did
she fall? Is the baby okay? Is she
okay?"

Rachel never stops reading her book. She shows no concern
about Jazmyn's well being.

"Benny calm down. They are just
observing her overnight to see if
they can stop the contractions.
The doctor doesn't want her to go
into labor it's a little too soon.
She still has a month and a half to
go. If she delivers the baby now, she
may have to stay in the hospital for
an extended period. They gave her
some medicine to stop the contractions
and made her comfortable. Right now,
she's stable and resting in her room.
I'm going home to get her some clothes
and toiletries. Then I'm coming back to
spend the night with her. I'll have
her call you when she wakes up. Don't
worry Benny, she's fine. Is my sister
there?"

"Okay please call me if there's any
changes, and yes your sister is here.
You wanna talk to her?"

"No, I will talk to her later. I have
to get home and back before it
gets too late. I don't want her here
by herself for too long," she says.

"Okay Noonie, thanks for letting
us know."

Uncle Benny replies.

"You're welcome. I know you worry.
She will be fine. I will take good care
of her."

Auntie Noonie enters my room. I want my phone back, but I'm
too sleepy to ask for it. There's no password on it. I hope she
doesn't look at it or go through it. Adults can be nosey when it
comes to your phone. I'm so drowsy I don't remember
anything except laying on the bed and that is it. I wake during
the night and it appears that Auntie Noonie went home. She
has an overnight bag that I know wasn't here before.

"Hey Punkin, how are you feeling?"

She rubs my arm.

Her hands are so soft and warm. They are exactly like my
mom's used to be. Oh, how I miss that lady.

"I'm okay."

I reply.

"Do you still feel contractions?"

"Not as much." I didn't feel like talking.

"I called your Uncle Benny and
Auntie Rachel to tell them what
was going on."

She informs me. I hear my phone vibrate. Auntie Noonie hands it to me. I look at the time. It's 10:30pm.

> *Sean - Hey sweetie, I was just checking on you. How are things with your Auntie?*
>
> *Jazzy - I'm so glad you text me. I haven't had my phone to let you know everything was fine and thank you again for ordering the car to get me to the airport.*
>
> *Sean - Remember, I told you anything for you.*
>
> *Jazzy - Why are you so nice to me?*
>
> *Sean - I like you.*
>
> *Jazzy - But I'm pregnant with someone else's baby.*
>
> *Sean – So.*
>
> *Jazzy - You don't care?*
>
> *Sean - Why should I? I think you are beautiful and smart.*
>
> *Jazzy - I'm also only sixteen years old.*
>
> *Sean - A very mature, beautiful sixteen-year old, it's only a problem if you start telling people.*
>
> *Jazzy - I would be in so much trouble if my family knew about you, but I like you so much too.*
>
> *Sean - They don't have to know. I'm yours not theirs.*

While I text him, I am thinking about never telling anyone about him. Mimi is the only person that knows a little about us. She keeps all my secrets.

The old man comments she makes are unnecessary, but I really like this dude. Malik is still my love, but I don't know about him being in my son's life. I fear for my life with him. Malik is too violent. He could hurt me, kill me or hurt our baby. I can't take that chance.

> *Sean - What are you doing now?*
> *Jazzy - I'm in the hospital.*
> *Sean - What? Why didn't you tell me*
> *that when I first text?*
> *Jazzy - Because I really wouldn't have*
> *told you if you hadn't asked*
> *how I was doing.*
> *Sean - Why? I care about you. I want*
> *to know what's going on with*
> *the baby.*

Here he goes again. I just don't get it. At the same time, it feels good to know he cares so much.

> *Jazzy - It's not your responsibility.*
> *He's my responsibility.*
> *Sean - He? It's a boy? For real?*

Why is he getting excited? He's not the father of my baby. We aren't even boyfriend and girlfriend. I've never even seen him in person. He's sweet and all, but I have so many decisions to make. I don't want him in my mess. Auntie Noonie is going to help me get on my feet so I can take care of me and my baby. I want to be on my own.

>   *Jazzy - Sean why are you getting so excited?*
>   *You're not the father. We never even*
>   *had sex.*
>   Sean - *Because I wanna be here for you*
>   *and the little peanut.*
>   *Jazzy - Peanut? Ugh! Anyway, you don't*
>   *have to be. I got this.*

Laying in this hospital bed is so uncomfortable. I wanted to go home to my own bed and sleep.

>   Sean - *Why are you in the hospital*
>   *sweetie?*

He is trying to change the subject. Great idea because I got this, like I said.

>   *Jazzy - I fell getting out of the shower*
>   *and started having pains. I guess*
>   *labor pains. They keep telling my*
>   *Auntie everything that's going*
>   *on with me. It's annoying. I'm*
>   *like I am the one having the baby*
>   *TALK TO ME!*
>   Sean - *Wow that's crazy they won't talk*
>   *to you. I hope you feel better. You*
>   *should probably be resting lil*
>   *mama. I'm gonna hit you in the*
>   *morning and check on you.*
>   *Jazzy - Okay thanks for checking on*
>   *me. You're very sweet, Sean.*

I decide to scroll my Instagram and see who is posting about their lives. What's everybody doing? The first post I see is Malik. He's in a picture with this hood rat girl that lives down the street. He's high and hugged up with her. I hate Malik and love him at the same time. He said he loves me, but I'm not sure I believe it. I need to talk to Mimi. On second thought, it's too late. I'll talk to her tomorrow. A nurse walks in and tells me everything is fine. She says, you'll be released first thing in the morning, but when you go home relax. You know that's a profound idea. I think I'll start right now, goodnight.

Chapter Nine

After my brief hospital stay, I am advised to take it easy. Dr. Smith doesn't necessarily say I need total bedrest, but the things she instructed me to do sounds like it. Nevertheless, there are a few school projects and papers I need to complete. I need to be ahead just in case he comes early. My life is going to be drastically changed; and I have no idea what it's like to study with a baby. In a little while, I will know first-hand. The other day I received a letter from the school. Auntie handed me the letter and stood right there to see what was inside. It was my report card. The school sends it online and by mail. I had straight A's. She looked at it. Her eyes got big and a big smile came over her face. Punkin! I'm so proud of you. I looked at her like it wasn't a big deal, that's what I do. I'm smart. You just didn't know it.

When my mother was alive, she used to always tell me how important my education was. Her words were, "You have to study hard Jazmyn and soak up all of the knowledge you can. You know why? Can't nobody take that away from you." Mama read a lot too and I like to quote some of the things she read. One of the things she would say is "Good Better Best, never let it rest, until your good is better and your better is best." It came from Elizabeth George's book, *A Woman After God's Own Heart.* I remember her saying that all the time. When school is in, I'm working to get the highest grades I can in every subject. I still want to make her proud.

"Jazmyn this is fantastic. Whoa girl,
I need to lay down. I'm feeling tired."

Auntie still doesn't look well.

"Auntie, are you feeling okay?"

"I feel really tired. I don't know
what's going on with my body.
I think I just need to slow down
and rest for the day. You need to
figure out what you are going to
cook for dinner tonight. We
have everything here so you
shouldn't pick anything new that
requires ingredients we don't have."

I love when Auntie teaches me how to plan my menus. She gave me a notebook to write all of my recipes, cooking instructions and other etiquette type stuff. I call it my Life Book. It's so cool. I usually read it after I finish my homework. Today, I finished my classes early. I can read my Life Book and text Sean when I'm done. I leave Auntie's room and walk down the hall to my room. Let me call Sean before I read. I dial his number. Wow, he doesn't answer. Text seems to be his only way of communication.

Jazzy - Hey Sean.
Sean - Hi whatchu doin?
Jazzy - I'm not doing anything.
Sean - You okay? Everything okay
with the baby?

Jazzy - Yes everything is good.
　　　　The baby is good. I'm just
　　　　getting so big I can't get
　　　　comfortable. I think my
　　　　Auntie is sick or something.
Sean - Why do you say that?
Jazzy - Because she keeps sleeping a
　　　　lot. She's barely eating. I made
　　　　breakfast this morning and she
　　　　ate a little bit of it, that's so
　　　　unlike her.
Sean - Have you asked her how she feels?
Jazzy - Yes, and she says she's just tired.
　　　　I'm worried about her.
Sean - Well keep an eye on her and if she
　　　　doesn't get better by tomorrow maybe
　　　　call the doctor. But I'm concerned
　　　　about you.
Jazzy - I'm okay, I just need to talk to my
　　　　aunt. I'll text you later.

I walk to Auntie Noonie's room and gently tap on her door.
She faintly replies.

"Come in Baby."

"Auntie can I talk to you for a minute?
I need to tell you about Malik."

"Sure, sit down."

I take a deep breath. As I look down at my hands.
I'm fidgety and nervous.

"Soooo, the reason I don't want
Malik to have anything to do with
the baby is because he is physically
abusive."

I struggled to get those words out.

"Oh, my goodness baby. Why
didn't you say anything when
I asked you about him?"

She perks up to listen. I start to cry. It seems like that's all I
do now. Everything I've been through begins to flood back in.
It is like highlights of Malik's abuse starts to play over in my
mind. I press my hands on my face to cover my crying eyes.
Auntie comes close and pulls me into a big hug. She strokes
my hair and she slightly rocks me to soothe me like my mom
used to do.

"Honey I'm so sorry you had
to go through that. You don't
have to give me details if
you don't want to."

"I'm okay talking to you. I told
my best friend."

She released me from the most comforting hug I had in a long
time.

"Go ahead whenever you are ready."

Auntie Noonie sits back. I wait a minute to get strong again.

> "He was so nice at the beginning.
> Then things started to change.
> It was like something switched
> in him. I would be at his house
> and look at his phone over his
> shoulder and he would go off on
> me. Sometimes he would even
> push me to the ground. He has
> grabbed me and put bruises on
> my arms. He has slapped me
> and left marks. It was terrible.
> Auntie, I don't know why I kept
> going back for more. I just know
> that I love him so much and don't
> want to lose him. The last time he
> put his hands on me, was right
> after I found out I was pregnant.
> That's when I knew I had to get
> out of there and never go back."

Auntie is very quiet and didn't interrupt. Near the end of my dialogue, or what looked like the end, she spoke.

> "So did you tell your Uncle or Rachel?"

> "You know I can't talk to her. I would
> never tell her anything."

> "Did they know you were seeing
> him? I'm thinking not, because
> you can't date, right?"

"No, I snuck over there for a long
time. They never knew. After a
while, I knew I couldn't say
anything because I would get into
trouble."

"How did you break it off with him?"

I squirm a little on her bed. I was so uncomfortable telling her
all of this. I don't want her to track him down and hurt him.
I didn't want her to call the police on him either. I utter,

"I'm just scared of everything.
I block him on my phone and
social media. I don't know if he
tries to call me or not. He sends
me messages from other numbers.
I don't respond normally, but one
text he acted like he was someone
else. He never verified, but I
know it was him."

"You're safe. Don't worry about him
getting to you here. I was once in an
abusive relationship. I was about
your age, but he really beat me badly.
I was in the hospital with broken ribs,
a broken arm and my face was cut up
from it. I won't go into details on
what he did, but it was bad. I had to
get the police involved."

This incident still haunts my aunt even though it was long ago.
Auntie continues.

> "One thing that we have in common
> is I got pregnant by 'The Abuser' too.
> The only difference is he beat me so
> badly I lost the baby within a month
> and a half of my delivery date."

Auntie Noonie says as her voice begins to fade lower and
lower into a whisper. My eyes are burning as I hold more
tears back. She cries a little but not loudly. She pauses.
I hand her a tissue so she can wipe her tears. I'm
feeling bad for her.

> "Auntie, I'm so sorry. I didn't know,"

> "It's okay honey. That was a long
> time ago and I'm all good now."

She gets off the bed, starts moving around, and goes
downstairs. I watch her and walk to my room.

> "I'm going to make dinner now,
> okay?"

She yells.

> "Okay, I'll be reading my
> Life Book!"

I yell back.

After falling asleep while reading my Life Book, my mother
comes to me in a dream.

"Hey baby girl, you are doing so good
eating right and learning from Noonie."

Mommy said. I was startled when I saw my mommy sitting on
the side of my bed. It felt real.

"Mommy you're here."

I hug her tightly but feel nothing.

"Yes, baby I'm here. Look, you are
almost a mom and I need to tell
you some things. It's going to be
very hard once my grandson gets
there. You will not get a lot of
sleep, juggling school, making
sure he's okay and taking care of
yourself. Please make sure you take
good care of yourself, that's very
important. Auntie is not going to
help you, not because she doesn't
love you, but because you must
learn motherhood on your own.
She's going to push responsibility
and you aren't going to like it.
You will be an amazing mom,
trust mommy. And most of all,
trust God."

"Mommy, I can't do this without you.
I need you here to show me how to be
an amazing mom like you were to me."

"You will be an amazing mom."

Mommy said with a proud smile. I tried to take in her smell by laying my head on her chest. It was a dream. Mommy used to always smell like fresh cut flowers. It was heavenly.

"Mommy?"

I say, then stop. I'm afraid I will wake up and she'll be gone.

"Yes baby?"

She responds.

That's mommy's soft voice. It just warms my heart. I want to hold on to that forever.

"I don't know Mommy, I just need
you here forever. I need your help."

It's so hard when she comes to me in a dream.

"Punkin, you got this. Trust me."

She states. I could feel Auntie trying to wake me up.

"Jazzy, baby, wake up. Dinner is
ready." Auntie says softly.

I wake up, don't see my mom and start crying uncontrollably.

"Heyyyy hey, what's going on?
Why are you crying?"

Auntie asks. With my face buried in my hands I try to stop crying. Things are so complicated; Malik is the father and he doesn't know. Sean is such a sweet person, but too old to be talking to. I'm out here on my own. I don't feel like I have anyone, even though I have Auntie. I still feel alone.

"Jazmyn talk to me. What's wrong?"

Once I pull myself together, I try to say what is hard to say.

"Auntie, I just don't know what's
going to happen. I need my mom.
Why did she have to die?"

"We can't answer why God took your
parents. We can only live the life that
we have right now and honor God.
There are decisions you made and
consequences you must live with.
You are having a baby honey.
Unfortunately, your mother isn't
here to help you. We are almost
there. Realistically, the baby could
come at anytime."

She stops and waits for me to speak, but I don't have any-thing to say. She really isn't helping. My heart is aching for my mother, no one can help me with that. I want my
mother. It's not fair.

"Auntie, she keeps coming to me in
my dreams and they feel so real. I
can smell her when I wake up. She
touches me and talks to me. I know
she's here at least in my dream it
feels too real. Why am I dreaming
about her?"

I look her in the eyes searching for an honest answer.

"She knows you need her. The only way
for you to hear what she is saying is to
come to you in your dreams. This is
another way God gives you a message
of comfort through your mother. God
is watching over us and he comforts us
when things are hard for us." I miss
my mother so much. We were best
friends."

"Really? You were best friends with
your mother? That's so cool. I
couldn't imagine that."

"Yes, my mother lived with me before
she died. When mama got sick, I went
and got her from Southern California
and brought her up here so, I could
care for her. I was married at the
time and my husband loved her just
as much as I did, if not more."

Auntie pauses as if in her own world for a minute.

"Okay baby, enough of this, let's
get some dinner. I'm starved."

Just like that Auntie Noonie leaves the room and heads
downstairs. I am left there in limbo wondering what just
happened. An intense conversation, then nothing. Oh well,
I guess it's time to eat. I go downstairs, eat dinner, go back to
my room and begin to text Sean.

Jazz - Hey there!

Sean doesn't answer right away as usual.

> *Jazz - I guess you don't want to talk
> to me right now.*
> *Sean - Baby why are you impatient.
> I'm right here.*
> *Jazz - Why do you take so long to
> answer me?*
> *Sean - I'm working.*
> *Jazz - Can you text right now?*
> *Sean - Yes*
> *Jazz - I'm bored.*
> *Sean- How are you doing?*
> *Jazz - I'm good. I just had a long
> deep conversation with my
> Auntie. She seems to be
> feeling better.*
> *Sean - Was it a good convo?
> Or was she teaching you
> a life lesson?*

> *Jazzy - No, I was telling her*
> *about my baby's father.*
> *She's been asking a lot*
> *of questions about him*
> *that I didn't want anyone*
> *to know.*
> *Sean - Why so secretive?*
> *Jazz - It's not nobody's business.*
> *He was very mean to me.*
> *Sean - Hang on, I have to pick up*
> *this trash.*

I don't remember exactly what he does for the airlines, but I don't recall picking up trash being included.

> *Sean - Okay I'm back.*

Upon his return, Uncle Benny calls me.

> *Jazz - Let me get back to you. I'm*
> *gonna talk to Uncle Benny.*
> *Sean - Okay.*

"Hi Uncle Benny!"

"Hey babygirl. How are you feeling today?'

"I'm feeling sleepy Uncle, all the time."

"Are you? The time is near for you to have the baby." He says.

"Yes, the doctor won't let me do much either, so I just sit around all day."

"Well, that's okay Punkin you have to rest up for my nephew. He may be a handful for you."

"Why you say that? I want him to be the perfect little angel for his mommy."

I laugh.

"Hang on Punkin, there's someone at the door."

He walks over to the door and opens it.

"Hey Shawn what's going on?"

"Hi Mr. Jackson, I'm finished with everything. Do you need anything else?"

"No Shawn, let me get your money. Come on in. You want something to drink, water? Soda?"

"No sir, I have water. Thank you."

"Punkin it was Shawn at the door.

"Shawn! Who is Shawn, Uncle Benny?"

"You know him, the young man who
does things around the house."

"Oh yeah, Uncle Benny may I
speak to him please? We go to
school together."

"Shawn my niece wants to
speak to you."

He hands Shawn the phone and walks away.

"Hi Shawn. This is Jazmyn.
I just wanted to thank you for
what you did when I was there
with Malik. You have no idea
how much you helped me."

"Oh no problem. I just happened
to be in the right place at the right
time."

"I just wanted to say thank you.
I appreciate it."

"You're welcome. Here's your
uncle."

He hands the phone to him.

"Thank you Mr. Jackson."

"You're welcome Shawn, and thank
you.

He hands him money and closes the door. Shawn counts his
money, while walking down the driveway.

"One hundred, one-fifty, two hundred,
two- fifty. Wow, Mr. Jackson really
takes care of me. Two hundred and fifty
dollars, but it still isn't better than
hearing Jazmyn's voice."

Chapter Ten

Buzzzzz! Buzzzz! There goes my phone again. He's frantically texting me like he has lost his simple little mind. He really gets on my nerves.

> Malik - *Jazzy I need to talk to you.*
> Malik - *Jazz baby I need to talk to you ASAP*
> Malik - *JAZMYN I HAVE SOME STUFF*
> *GOING ON I NEED TO TALK TO*
> *YOU.*

Maybe Mimi knows something about where she is.

"Hello." Mimi answers.

"Whas up Mimi, this Malik."

"Oh, hey Malik."

"You seen Jazz?"

"No, I haven't seen her Malik."

I know she's lying. Jazz tells her everything.

"What do you want with her?"

"I just need to talk to her and she's not answering my calls or text. It's been a long time."

"Well, if I talk to her, I will let you know. Bye."

"Mimi, wait!."

"What Malik."

"Is she pregnant with my baby?"

"Boy! What are you talking about? No, she's not pregnant with your baby! Where did you get that from?"

"Cuz, I heard her say something about her baby and I can see she's gaining weight, so don't lie. Is she pregnant?"

"Malik she ain't pregnant!"

"SHE IS AND AFTER I FIND HER IMMA COME FOR YOU, LIAR!"

I hang up in her face. Liar! She's trying to keep me from my baby. I'll get with her after I find Jazmyn. I need to be there for her and the baby. I don't understand why she left. She said she loved me. I promised I would never hurt her again. My phone! Maybe that's her texting me.

> *Omar - Hey man we gotta do this*
> *thang tonight.*
> *Malik - What time?*
> *Omar - Same time. Talk to you.*

Omar rarely sends a text. He says things can be traced. We have a big drug deal tonight with one of the Jamaican dudes. Omar finally trusts me to handle things. I'd better live up to his expectations, cause this game ain't no joke. That's why he gave me some heat the other day. I better get ready. He's picking me up in an hour. This black tee should be cool to wear, along with black dickies, black tennis shoes and a black beanie. I'll put the gun in the back of my pants in the waist band. He's here already? That sounds like him talking to Big Mama.

"Hey Big Mama."

"Hey Omar. Watchu doin here?"

"I can't come over no mo?"

"It's late. You don't be comin' over here late."

"Well, me and Malik got business."

He says and walks away.

"Y'all up to no good. I can tell. You done already corrupted Malik."

When Omar gets to my room, he hands me a backpack. I look inside and it's full of money.

I put it on and look at how he's dressed. Omar is wearing jeans and a white tee with Tupac on it. Why am I dressed like a thief? I'm very nervous because I've never done anything like this before. I've sold a few drugs here and there in small doses, but this is big. We leave the house and hop in the car.
I wait to ask questions when we get in the car. There has been a black Honda Accord parked out front for the past few months. The windows are tinted very dark so I can't tell if anyone is in it or not. It's just parked in the same place everyday. Really weird. I have to ask Big Mama if she noticed anything.

In the car Omar starts to give me instructions.

> "Okay this is how this is going
> down. I'm gonna pull up to the spot.
> The guy is gonna get in the car,
> give you the drugs, you give him
> this backpack and we out. Don't
> talk to him. Just hand him the
> money."

> "Okay, Got it!"

I say trying not to sound like a punk. As we drive to the spot, I'm going over my move in my mind. Omar interrupts my mental rehearsal.

> "Aye Man, give me your gun.
> I wanna switch it out with this
> one."

He hands me a different gun. It feels different. I put the new one in my waist band. It's much lighter than the first one he gave me. Almost feels like a cap gun. We pull up in front of this building. It's painted all black.

153

The door is black and so inconspicuous that I didn't see it until we stop in front of it. It's an industrial neighborhood where buildings line both sides of the street. The Jamaican comes out looking both ways as he walks to the car.

Once inside the car, I notice a black SUV slowly driving up beside us. I look over to see who is inside. "The Jamaican," taps my shoulder and presents two bricks to me. As I begin to take the backpack off, bullets begin to pierce through the car. POP! POP! POP! POP! Glass shatters all around us. I duck down under the dashboard, and pray I don't die tonight. I reach for my gun in case I make it out of the car alive. The shots last for what feels like an hour, but in reality it's just minutes. Then, there is silence. I hear my door open. I look over at Omar. His lifeless body is slumped over the steering wheel. Blood flows from his head, mouth and other places. His body is full of holes. Suddenly, I'm jerked from the car and something black is placed over my head. I can't see anything. My hands are quickly tied. Who can this be? Is my first thought. They put me in a car and drive off.

> "Hey! Please don't hurt me!"

No one answers.

> "I don't wanna die tonight please!
> What do you want me to do? I'll
> do whatever you want me to do!"

I scream.

> "Shut up!" A deep voice yells.
> It's a male's voice and he doesn't
> sound familiar at all.

"Where are you taking me? Please!"

I'm begging from what feels like the back seat. I feel the car slow down and then stops. My car door opens and they yank me out. They untie my hands and drive off.

"Hey! Where am I?" I yell.

I snatch the sack off my head. I try to see the make and model of the car. It was too far to figure out, but further down the street I'm sure they were in a black Honda. When I look around, I realize that I'm in front of Big Mama's house. Whoever it was knew where I lived.

Big Mama is sleeping for sure and so are the kids in the house. Mookie stays up late sometimes or at least tries to. I'd better slip into my room, so I won't wake anyone up. Once in my room, I start to pick glass out of my hair. I need to change my clothes too.

While changing, I hear someone banging on the front door. I grab my gun, my hoodie, the backpack and climb out the window. I run through the backyard and begin to hop fences to get out of the neighborhood. Wow! You really have to be in some kind of shape to be a Drug Dealer. I must find someplace to hide out, so I can rest awhile. If only I knew where Jazmyn was. I need her right now. Maybe I'll walk to L.T.'s house. I should be safe there.

Upon arriving to his home, I realize I had left my cellphone and wallet at Big Mama's house. I'll tap on his window to get his attention. It's nothing new for us. I tap on his window during the day also. He comes to the window and opens it.

"What man?" LT whispers.

It's one o'clock in the morning and everyone in his house is asleep.

> "Hey man, I need a place to crash
> for the night."

He opens the window wide enough for me to climb in. He throws me a pillow and gets back in bed without a word. That's what I love about him. He doesn't ask a bunch of questions. He is always there when I need him. I grab an extra blanket from the closet, put my hood on my head, lay on the floor and try to sleep. I look at the window, after laying there for what feels like a full night. Sunlight starts to break through the slits in the blinds. I'm not sure I slept at all. When L.T. wakes up, I need him to get me to my house. But, judging by the way things went down last night, living at Big Mama's isn't possible or safe anymore. I'm sure she won't want me there. I need a plan. For now, I will try to sleep. I keep asking myself, who snatched me out of the car? Who shot up the car? Why was someone trying to kill us? I'm glad I at least grabbed my gun. Protection is needed in case I run into those fools; but who are the fools? L.T. wakes up. He picks up his phone to check the time and says, "So what's up?"

> "It went down last night the
> wrong way. It's all bad. L.T.,
> they killed Omar and the
> Jamaican."

> "What? Didn't you and Omar
> go together?"

> "Yeah."

L.T. walks over to the window and looks out and says.

"Malik, you have to get out
of here. People know we're boys.
This is the first place they'll
come looking for you."

"I know L.T."

"Well, why did you come here?
You're putting my family in
jeopardy"

"I know. I couldn't think of
anywhere else. Can you take
me to Big Mama's and drop
me off in Orange County?"

"Let me shower, get dressed
and we can roll."

He gets some clothes and leaves the room.

In the meantime, I'm thinking about my next move without
my phone I can't look up any hotels. No one will look for me
in Orange County though. L.T. returns to the room after a very
lengthy shower.

"Imma have to drop you off
around the corner from Big Mama's.
My homeboy just text me and confirmed
your story. It's all kinds of cops there."

My heart begins to beat very fast.

I picture Omar slumped over the steering wheel with all the blood everywhere. How did I make it out alive? My focus now is getting in and out of Big Mama's house with no problems. I need my wallet and cellphone.

"Yo dog, you hear me?"

"Yeah T, I hear you. We need to go."

We get into L.T.'s loud car and go to Big Mama's. Good thing he drops me off around the corner because there are cars everywhere. People hanging outside in front of the house. I walk back to the car and get in.

L.T. says.

"You got your stuff that fast?"

"Naaaahhh it was too many people like your boy told you."

"Malik, you can't go back there right now. I'll spot you some ends so you can stay somewhere."

"I'm cool L.T."

Malik sighs.

"Just take me to Katella and Valley View in the OC."

"I got you Malik, but what's on
your mind, you cool?"

"Last night was crazy yo. Today
is even crazier to see all those
people in front of Big Mama's
house. Of all those people I
recognized only one person.
That kid Jazz calls Lawnboy.
He was sitting on his bike
talking to Mookie near the
sidewalk. I didn't know they
talked. Why would they even
be talking? Mookie is in
middle school, eighth grade,
not high school. That dude is a
weirdo. "Can we stop at Target
I need to get a couple of things?"

"Fa sho."

I realize I still have the backpack full of money with me. I have
more than enough to hold me. I take it off, look in, take out ten
one hundred dollar bills and hand them to LT.

"Here's a few dollars for helping
me L.T., Thanks."

He doesn't take it and says,

"Malik! We're cool. I'm good.
This is a thousand dollars!"

"Take it. You've been a true
friend and I really need one
right now."

I get out the car and walk into Target."

Chapter Eleven

The phone wakes me up. Buzzzzz! Buzzzz! Buzzzzz! Buzzzz! It is back to back text. I'm irritated now. I try to focus on the words I read.

> *Mimi - Jazz pick up I need to talk to you. It's important.*
> *Mimi - JAZZZZZ I NEED TO TALK TO YOU WHERE ARE YOU?*
> *Mimi - Jazmyn, call me.*
> *Mimi - Call me.*
> *Mimi - Call when you get a chance.*

I keep reading through and finally I get to the dreaded message.

> *Mimi - Jazzmyn I don't know where you are, but Malik has been shot. He's dead.*

I gasp, "Oh nooooooo!"

I start to scream.

"Ohhhhhh nooooo!"

Auntie Noonie comes running into the room.

"What's going on Jazz? What's wrong?"

"I hold my stomach and cry."

I'm thinking to myself, what is going on with Malik. I never wanted him to die. I just wanted him to get himself together. I fall into Auntie's arms and sob uncontrollably. My first thought is how do I go on? How do I explain to our son that his father was shot and killed? My tears last for a while and Auntie just holds me the entire time. I finally stop and get up to go to the restroom. I see spotting in my panties and start to cramp.

"Auntieeeee!!!"

I scream.

"Something is wrong!!!

Auntie comes in the bathroom and I'm sitting on the floor holding my stomach trying to catch my breath.

"Let's go to the hospital now! Can you make it downstairs?"

I'm crying again. I just shake my head and she helps me off the floor. We walk to the garage. She helps me into the car and calls Dr. Smith.

"Something is wrong and the contractions are back. Meet us at the hospital."

We get to the hospital in record time.

"Let's get you in a wheelchair young
lady. Dr. Smith is waiting for you
upstairs in labor and delivery."

I can't speak. The contractions are coming faster than before.
Auntie Noonie is just running alongside the wheelchair with
all of my junk in her arms. I'm trying to breathe through the
contractions. My phone is going off again. I can't answer. I
don't want to talk right now anyway. The admissions process
is smooth, but the contractions are kicking my butt. They are
too close together and HURT. I can't tell when they stop. This
pain is too much to handle. I can't even change into the gown
the nurse laid on the bed. Auntie helps me get into my gown.
The doctor comes in to check me. She has a shocked look on
her face.

"Doctor, is everything okay?"

"Yes, it's time to have a baby boy."

She leaves for a few seconds and comes back in with another
nurse. While the nurses are prepping me, I can hear Auntie
talking to Uncle Benny on the phone. I can also hear my phone
ringing, which has been ringing since I got to the hospital.
Once the pain got too bad, I couldn't hear anything.

"Wait Doctor! It's not time. It's
too early. He's not due for
another month."

"Well, your baby wants to come
a little early. We don't have time
for anything. It's still safe for
him to come into the world now."

Dr. Smith says.

> "I FEEL LIKE I HAVE TO
> PUUUUUSSSSHHHHH!"

> "Okay Auntie, stand on the other
> side and hold her leg. The nurse
> is going to hold your other leg
> Jazmyn. Now, when you feel
> another contraction, I want you
> to push."

She says while sitting like a catcher on a baseball team. I push hard. Stop. Breathe a little. Push hard. Stop. Breathe a little more, then take a deep breath and push and feel the baby slide right out. Dr. Smith talks me through the whole thing. Once Jayson is here, I immediately feel relief. Auntie has tears in her eyes watching them place him on my naked chest. My first thought is why would they put him on me with all the slimy bloody stuff on him. That is so nasty. Then I hear him crying. It's my baby. I hold him and fall instantly in love.

> "It's okay baby, mommy's here."

I'm not paying attention to the fact that the doctor is still down there. She begins to push on my stomach. I'm like Dr. Smith, what are you doing? The baby is right here. We don't need to push anymore.

> "Jazmyn, I'm getting the placenta
> out. It might be a little painful, but
> once that's out, I'll stitch you up
> and it's over."

I take a deep breath to resist the pain.

"Okay."

The placenta slides out, without a problem. The stitching is another story.

"Jazmyn, so we have about 20 tiny stitches to do."

"Wait, what? Stitches?"

I ask the nurse who was trying to take the baby from me.

"What are you doing?"

I look at her. The doctor is speaking very calmly and softly which brings my anxiety down.

"Jazmyn, look at me honey. The baby has to be checked and cleaned up. The nurse will take him right over there and check him. She will clean him up, put a diaper on him, and give him back to you. Your Auntie Noonie will be over there with them if you are not comfortable with him being away."

Dr. Smith explains. Auntie is already watching what they are doing. My insides are feeling weird. I begin to moan which gets the doctor's attention.

"Okay, this will be quick. Just breathe deep and you won't feel much."

I just close my eyes hoping it will go fast. Holding my legs up and being exposed felt uncomfortable. My phone is still making noise. Who is blowing me up like that? I don't talk to that many people since I don't live in So Cal anymore.

"All done," she says.

She puts my gown down. Auntie is slowly rocking the baby. Exhaustion fades and excitement fills my heart. I want to hold my baby and sleep. The nurse comes over and informs me that they are moving me into my room. They put the baby in what looks like a clear plastic square crate and rolls him to the room. Auntie has all my belongings and hers. It's almost like we are moving into the hospital. Once I am settled in my room, I want to hold my baby. My fatherless baby.

> "Auntie, can you pass me Jayson please? And my phone. I want to talk to my best friend about what happened to his daddy."

Jayson is wrapped up like a burrito. He can't move. They said I have to keep him wrapped like that so he can feel like he's still in the womb. It's comforting. He feels like a football. I smile as I look at this miracle from God.

> "Dear Lord, it's me Jazmyn. Ummmm, I'm not sure what to say right now. There are so many things going on in my life. You blessed me with this beautiful baby boy, but on the same day his father was taken away from us. What do I do now Lord?"

I stop because I don't know what else to say. I hold my baby tight and cry into his blanket. I don't cry for too long. I gather myself and stop crying long enough to call Mimi.

"Hello," Mimi answers.

"Mimi?"

"Jazz you okay?"

"No, but my baby is beautiful. He looks just like his dad. That makes it hard."

"Oh, Jazz I'm so sorry. Really I am. Let me know how I can help from here?"

"There's nothing any one can do. But do you know any details of what happen?"

"What happened?"

"Yes, what happen to Malik! How was he killed? Why is he dead? What am I supposed to do?" I start to cry.

"Jazzy I'm sorry. Please, please don't cry.
I heard he was with Omar and someone
shot up the car. Omar walked away, but
the Jamaican dude in the backseat and
Malik didn't. Apparently, Malik was
driving."

I stop crying when I hear her say he was driving. Malik doesn't
know how to drive. That's why he was always riding with
someone or walking. I need to get some more information.
This doesn't sound right.

"Who told you this? Malik couldn't
even drive."

"I was at lunch and heard some
football players talking about it."

"Something isn't right. I have to
go and feed my baby. I'll talk
to you later."

I'm too tired to think about all of this anymore. It's just too
much. Having a baby takes everything out of a woman. I never
knew I would be this tired. Baby Jay is quiet and sleeping. I
think I'll join him and get some sleep too.

Chapter Twelve

I wake to Baby Jay screaming like someone pinched him. Auntie placed him in my arms. I have no idea what I'm supposed to do. Before Auntie starts her instructions, the nurse comes in to help me breastfeed him. I just want him to stop crying. She gives me so many instructions and I'm so tired. I'm not sure how to do anything. Before I can say anything, the nurse puts him on my breast. Jayson is eating.

> "Jazmyn, I will be back a little later to check on you. Try to breastfeed him on both sides so you are sure he's full."

The nurse instructs me.

> "Thank you."

That's all I can get out as Baby Jay sucks on my breast. It's the weirdest feeling. A little mouth tugging on my nipple and food coming out for him, amazing. God is so amazing the way He made our bodies. Auntie stood silently next to me watching my every move. Baby Jay latches right on and starts drinking away, but it hurts so bad. The nurse looks at everything.

"Okay it looks perfect. You're
doing a great job. I'll come
back and check on you."

"Okay. Hey why am I still cramping?
It hurts badly."

I'm so stressed.

"Well, having a baby is very traumatic
for your body. Everything has to go
back to normal and that takes time.
In the meantime, your insides have to
get back to normal. You will cramp as
your uterus goes back to its regular
size. Don't worry it's normal."

She leaves my room. I begin to think about my son and the
name he will have for the rest of his life. Jayson Benjamin
Jackson, that's his name, and I'm his mother.

After sleeping for a few hours with no interruptions, I"m back
to reality. I'm really a mommy. This little boy is going to
depend on me for everything. I receive another weird text
from a number I don't know.

> *Weird number - Is this Jazmyn?*
> .   *Jazzy - Who dis?*
> *Weird number - I need to speak to*
> *you Jazmyn.*
> *Jazzy - Not until you tell*
> *me who you are.*

I put the phone down to take care of my baby. There is no time for games right now. Malik is gone so it can't be him trying to talk to me anymore. I think about Malik being dead again and start to cry uncontrollably. Auntie comes to my bedside. She takes Baby Jay and begins to speak to me.

> "Look, you are going to have
> to suck this up with Malik
> because your main concern
> is this baby right here. He
> needs all of you right now."

> "He was my kid's father! I can't
> just suck it up and forget about
> him!"

I yell at her. The nurse enters. She can hear me yelling.

> "Is everything okay?"

I can't respond. Auntie Noonie tells her.

> "Yes, everything is fine. We just
> received some bad news."

This is too much for me right now. I don't know what to do. I start to have a hard time breathing. It was like I couldn't catch my breath. My breathing became progressively faster and faster. I dropped my phone and grabbed my chest.

> "Nurse! Doctor! I need some
> help here!"

Auntie yells out the door. The nurse runs in. She leans my bed back and tries to ask me questions.

"Jazmyn, listen to me honey. I need
you to focus on my voice. Can
you talk to me?"

"I can't,- can't- catch- my- breath."

I try hard to catch my breath.

"Okay, I'm going to get some
oxygen for you. Hold on, you
will be fine honey."

This nurse is super nice. She is the same one that helped me
breastfeed. Just listening to her voice calmed me a little, but
I can't get control of my breathing. She covers my nose and
mouth with an oxygen mask and kept trying to calm me down.
Finally, I'm able to breathe like I normally do.

"Ms. Jackson?"

The nurse asks while looking at Auntie Noonie.

"No, Ms. Dueberry, but call me
Angela please."

"Oh, okay Angela, what can
I do to help Jazmyn?"

"Yes, her baby's father was tragically
killed today. She just read some text
messages from friends informing her
of his death."

The nurse is stunned and puts her hand over her mouth.

"I'm so sorry. Is there anything I
can do? I can have a therapist
converse with her about it."

"Oh yes please have a therapist
come in and talk to her."

"I was a teenage mom. I know
it's hard."

She says. She leaves and the baby begins to cry. I'm fast asleep
with the oxygen on. Auntie picks him up and rocks him. She
tries to wake me up to feed him but can't. The nurse enters the
room and Auntie Noonie asks her about formula.

"Can we give him formula if
she's not waking up?"

"Let's give her a little more time.
We'll try to wake her in thirty
minutes. If we can't wake her, I
will bring formula in so you can
feed him; but it's extremely
important that he feeds on
breastmilk.

"Thank you, and what's your
name again?"

"Oh, I thought I wrote it on the
board. My name is Dezi. I'm
the CNA and Amanda is the RN."

I start to wake up, but I'm still a little groggy.

"Hey baby girl, you want to
breastfeed the baby?"

Auntie asks.

"No." I turn my head away.

She is holding the baby toward me.

"Jazzy, your baby needs you now more
than ever. Remember, you said you
wanted to breastfeed him so he would
receive the best nutrition."

Auntie Noonie states. I don't say anything. I don't know
what I want.

"Jazzy, let me help you get ready
to feed him. He's hungry and
will be screaming in a minute if
you don't start now."

"Can you ask the nurse for formula
and you feed him?"

I turn my entire body away from her. Nurse Dezi returns.

"Are you ready to feed Jayson again?"

I shake my head no without turning around.

"She said to ask you for formula."

"Okay, I'll go get a bottle for him.
Just remember, it may make his little
tummy hurt."

Instead of leaving, Dezi walks over to me and says,

"Jazmyn you know your milk is so
much better for him. He needs you
right now or you will need a pump
to keep your milk going."

"Can you get the formula please?
I don't want to breastfeed right
now."

My heart literally feels like it is crushing inside my body. No
Malik ever again. What do I do with this empty feeling? How
do I go on? Even though he was abusive, and I didn't want
anything to do with him, he was the father of my child; and I
still love him. I only love him. What do I tell my son when he
starts to ask for his father? This is so painful. Dezi came back
with a tiny bottle that looks like it's for a baby doll. Auntie
feeds, burps, and changes his diaper. While sitting in the
rocker, Auntie Noonie rocks him and sings softly. She is in
love. After a few hours the therapist knocks on the door. I have
no idea who it is, but it is a woman dressed in a business suit,
so I know she's a therapist. I start looking at the TV, but not
really watching it. She has a badge pinned to her with the
hospital's logo on it. So, I guess she is supposed to be here.

"Hi! Jazmyn? I'm Doctor Paradise.
I'm a therapist here at the hospital.
I understand that you have just
had a baby. I also understand that
you've received some horrific news
as well."

I say nothing. I just lay back as if she wasn't there.

"I'm here to help you. We are
going to talk about the news
you've received and how you
feel about it."

"I don't want to talk about it.
Why do I have to talk to
someone about it? He's dead!
I don't want to talk."

"I understand your feelings, but
with a new baby and the news
of his father being killed on the
same day can be pretty
traumatic."

If this lady does not leave me alone. I don't want to talk.
Malik is dead. He's dead. I will never talk to him again. I will
never be able to say I don't want to talk to him. I don't get to
make a decision when Jayson is five that he needs to have a
relationship with his dad. Instead, I will be telling my son his
dad is dead. He will never meet him. What does this lady, Dr.
Paradise want me to tell her?

"Jazmyn, can you turn this way
please and face me?"

"For what? My kid's father is
dead! What are you suppose
to do? Bring him back?"

"No, talking about it will help you process
your feelings and give you the opportunity
to sort through them. You will be able to
make better decisions for you and your son."

"I'm feeling fine. I don't need you."

I forget Auntie Noonie is in the room. She suddenly makes her
presence known.

"Excuse me, Dr. Paradise, is it?"

"Yes, Dr. Paradise."

"Okay good, can you step
outside with me please?"

I don't budge. I'm not talking to the lady. Auntie talks to the
doctor on the other side of the door.

"I appreciate you trying to get through
to my niece, but maybe it's a little too
soon. I thought it would be a good
idea, but it's too much for her."

"Well, she needs to start talking about
her feelings as soon as possible to
process and understand what's going
on."

"Okay I understand, but maybe I jumped
the gun in calling for help. Let me be
with her and I will let the nurse know
when you can come back."

When she returns to the room it is like she brought my sadness
back. Malik is my one and only love. No matter what he did to
me that's what he is and now he's gone. Auntie gently places
her hand on my leg. Speaking softly she says,

"Babygirl, I know this is hard
and devastating, but Baby Jay
is gonna need all of you right
now. I can't stress that enough.
I can help you through this,
but you have to let me."

I'm in so much pain I can't even move. My heart and my
insides, where Baby Jay once lived, are in severe pain.

"Can you get the nurse please?
I'm in a lot of pain."

I hear Jayson crying. I can't get up because the pain in my
lower stomach is so bad. I don't remember anything after that.
I fall asleep. My mom is back in my dream. She is in the room
looking over Baby Jay and smiling. This time there is a light
behind her. It appears to be a soft white halo.

"Jazmyn he's beautiful."

"Mommy. He is huh? He's perfect.
I named him after daddy and
Uncle Benny."

"I know, baby. That was very
honorable of you. Your dad
is very proud of you."

"Where is he? How come he
hasn't come to me in my
dreams?"

"He will come, just not right
now. I came to talk to you again."

"Mommy sit down right here.
There's room like last time."

"No baby I can't sit, listen to me.
You remember when we used to
go to church every Sunday as a
family?"

"Yes. I miss that. Uncle Benny and
Auntie Rachel don't go to church
every Sunday, just sometimes."

"Now that you are a mother it's even more important for you to start going to church. The church is for you to learn about the "Word of God" and be in a place where other people believe what you believe. You have to read your bible and learn things for yourself. You have to teach my grandson about the Love of God. The last thing I want to tell you is how much I love you baby and how proud I am of you. You will be a great mother. Remember to rely on your instincts. Always pray, God will give you guidance and answers to whatever you are going through. Those instincts are whispered messages from God for your guidance. Always give thanks for all He has done for you. You will be blessed more than you can ever imagine if you just stay in God's Word. You have another life to keep safe and take care of. Listen to your Auntie Noonie. She's full of wisdom. She may not have children, but trust me, her knowledge goes far and wide. Don't hesitate to talk to her. I know you miss me baby. I miss you, but life constantly moves forward; and you don't have time to look back. God saved you from the accident because He needs you here for a very important task. It's up to you to pray. It's up to you to seek God's wisdom to understand what you are called to do."

I start to cry because this doesn't feel like her other visits. This sounds more like farewell. Why is she telling me this? Why is she saying to pray? I stopped praying because God took my parents. I'm alone because He took them. I have had to live without my parents. I miss them every day. I miss homemade pancakes for breakfast that my mother made. I miss sitting down with my daddy and reading with him. I miss my room and my bed. I miss everything. I'm just not sure what's going to happen. Auntie Noonie says my time is limited here. I wish my parents were here. This is so hard.

My mom interrupts my thoughts.

> "Baby I have to go now. I love you
> and remember what I've said."

I reach out to touch her hand, but she disappears. I cry and cry and cry, but I am still asleep. Auntie Noonie wakes me up again. She just holds me close like she knows what went on in my dream. My heart hurts so much. I need my mommy so much right now. Baby Jay starts to cry, I guess he's hungry again. This boy eats so much. I'm tired and feel so empty inside. Auntie passes him to me, surprisingly enough he latches right on and gobbles up whatever is in my right breast. He startles me when he begins to scream again.

> "Auntie, why is he crying like this?"

She comes over and takes him from me. She quiets him a little. I think it's because of all the walking, rocking and talking she does with him. When she places him back in my arms he starts to scream again.

> "Put him on your other breast.
> He may still be hungry."

I put him on the other side. Baby Jay starts sucking right away. He's hungry.

> "Little man, mommy has to get to know what to do for you. It's gonna be me and you. I will be everything you need to survive. Just like now. You need me for life. I'm here. I will never leave you. I love you Baby Jay. You are my entire world."

I whisper to him. Here he is Jayson Benjamin Jackson. My baby with jet black straight hair. The light brown wrinkly skin looks like Uncle Benny's skin, but his face looks just like Malik. I'm glad I named him after the two most important men in my life. I think my daddy would be so proud of his grandson. I just don't know how I will get over this empty feeling. I want to know what it means when he cries. I want to know why he's crying. I want to be the perfect mom.

> "I need to go to the bathroom. Is Amanda available?"

I say into the intercom. Quickly another nurse enters my room.

> "She's busy with a patient and asked me to check on you."

She says with a very hospitable smile.

> "What's your name?" I ask.

"Oh…I'm Nancy."

"Okay, I need help getting up, please."

I carefully swing my legs over the side of the bed and slide
off onto the floor. My legs feel a little wobbly at first.
Nancy holds my arm for support. Thank God for the socks
with the rubber on the bottom or I would have slid to the floor.
I feel so weird inside my body. I can't describe it. My lower
stomach is cramping a little but as I move around, the pain
subsides. The act of using the bathroom is a bit painful, too.
Everything is painful. I guess I'll have to get through it. While
I'm still standing, I need to change the baby's diaper. Being a
new mother shows as I try to change him. It takes me a few
minutes to figure out the right way to place the diaper. Does
the tape go in the back to secure the front? I think this is how
you do it. If it stays on, I did it correctly. If it doesn't, we'll
just have to keep doing until it does. Too bad Jay has to endure
my lack of changing skills. He always screams the entire time
I'm doing this. He even peed on my neck while I struggled to
get him right.

> "Come on baby, Mommy is trying
> to get this on you the right way."

Nancy interrupts.

> "So, what you can do is put a wipe
> over his private while you change
> him. That way you won't get wet
> in the face while you change him.
> Jayson can pee at any time. Cool
> air can make him start peeing.
> You want to wipe him well and
> do his diaper like this."

She lifts him up by two legs like a chicken, slides the diaper under his bottom and before I could blink twice, she is passing him to me.

"Wow, you're fast. I don't think I will ever do it that fast. I just don't want him to pee on me. That's pretty nasty."

"Honey, pee is the least of your worries. He will poop on you, vomit on you and anything else that will come out of his body. You are a mom now, so you get it all. Let me tell you it's the most rewarding thing in the world. Jazmyn, you have brought another human being in the world that will look to you for everything. Remember that in everything you do. Every decision you make, think about your son first; and make sure it won't affect him in a negative way. Pictures on social media can be retrieved at any time. They never go away. Make sure you are posting appropriate stuff because you are a mother first. I will say it again, you are a mother first. Let me help you back in bed. Get your rest because you have his life ahead of you. If he's sleeping. You sleep too. Like now, put him down or let Auntie hold him and you get some sleep."

I scoot on the bed backwards trying to get comfortable. It wasn't easy but I found a sweet spot in the bed and tried to relax. Before I knew it, I was asleep.

Chapter Thirteen

After spending the night in the hospital and bringing my son into the world the nurses prepare me to go home. I'm nursing Baby Jay when Dr Smith enters the room.

"Good morning, Jazmyn."

"Hi Dr. Smith."

"Jazmyn, how are you feeling?"

"I'm feeling good. I don't have a lot of pain down there anymore."

"Good, when the baby is done eating, I need to check something and if all is well you will be able to go home today. Push your call button when you're done nursing."

"Okay."

She leaves the room and I continue to nurse Baby Jay. When I touch his skin, it is so soft, but wrinkly. I caress his soft skin while he tightens his fist.

I take his balled fist and stretch his fingers out. I examine the tiny transparent fingernails and the mini fingers. Such a precious gift, Jayson is to me. Lord, thank you. His hands are just like Malik's. His legs are tightly curled. He's still in the same position as when he was inside me. I am so in love with this little boy that I don't know what to do. I push the call button and the nurse brings in a wheelchair. They assist Baby Jay and I into it. They take us to the car, where Auntie Noonie had already purchased a baby seat, to begin our journey home.

Being home now feels so good. I get to sleep in my own bed. But first I want to talk to Auntie about what I've been thinking about.

"Auntie, can I ask you a question?"

"Of course, you can ask me anything."

"Are you saved?" I ask.

"I am saved, but I don't have a church home anymore."

"Do you really read your bible and pray daily?"

"Girl, yes."

The short answers gave me the impression she didn't want to really discuss it, but I am so curious about it. Auntie Noonie goes downstairs to cook dinner. I want to talk to Mimi and catch up with her.

"Hello."

Mimi and I greet each other at the same time.

"Hey girl. What are you doing?"

I ask.

"No, the question is what are you doing, new mom?"

"I'm breastfeeding Jayson. Have you heard more about Malik?"

"No, I haven't. I know people have been texting you about him."

I switched breasts while we are talking. As Jayson is moving to the other side, he's screaming bloody murder like he's starving. Mimi asks,

"What are you doing to him? Why is he screaming like that?"

"Oh, he gets mad when I interrupt his eating. All I'm doing is switching to the other breast so he can keep eating. He's greedy girl."

"What is it like being a mom, Jazz?"

Mimi asks.

"It's a trip so far. I can't believe there's
a whole human being depending on
me for everything. I mean everything.
His life depends on me. Doesn't
that sound insane?"

"Yes, I can't imagine. Daniel wants
to get me a dog and I'm freaking out
over that. Besides, my mom said I
can't have one. Just the thought of
all the rules my mom would have if
I got a dog. I was like Daniel, don't
get me anything. Girl, my moms is
trippin' again. I have to go."

"Why does she trip on you like that?"

"Jazz, I don't know."

"I wish you could come out here and visit
me. I want to see my friend. It gets pretty
lonely up here. Sean said he would come
visit once I had the baby, but I'm not sure
how Auntie Noonie would take it. We
haven't had a conversation about Sean yet."

"Still texting that old man, huh?"

"Anyway, I thought about Malik's
grandmother, Big Mama. I wonder
if she would want to see her great
grandbaby. I'm not sure if I should
reach out or not."

Mimi interrupted my thoughts.

> "Are you going to let Malik's grandmother
> see the baby? I heard she was really upset
> when he died. It might make her feel good
> to know that a piece of Malik is still on
> earth."

> "Yeah, maybe. I can't believe he
> died the day his son was born.
> Maybe I will attend the funeral
> if Auntie Noonie lets me out of
> the house. It may be too soon.
> I don't really want any drama
> either."

Auntie yells.

> "Jazmyn! Come eat dinner!"

> "Okay girl, I have to go and eat.
> Auntie Noonie doesn't like me
> taking forever to get downstairs.
> She likes to serve the food hot
> and eat it hot."

> "Okay, take care of my nephew."

> "I will see to that. Call you tomorrow."

After dinner I take a nice hot shower. It feels so good. It has
been a long time since I had one too. I felt so nasty. I get out
the shower and find Baby Jay fast asleep.

Lord, thanks again. For the first time in months, I am able to sleep the way I want to. As I begin to sink deeply into my rest, my daddy comes to me for the first time in my dream.
He is standing by my window and it seems like he is far away from me.

"Daddy is that you?"

"Yes, Sweetpea it's me."

I just start to cry. I miss my daddy so much. I can't even catch my breath. I'm crying so hard, but he doesn't come closer.

"Daddy, I am so sorry."

He just stands there saying nothing. I can't figure it out.

"Daddy, will you talk to me?"

"I will. You look beautiful honey. I can't believe my baby has a baby."

"Yeah, but I know I disappointed you. I'm sorry Daddy."

"You're okay. I had many hopes and dreams for my baby, but there's still time for you to achieve them. Don't let this setback deter you from your Godly path. You can show your baby your strength. You can still finish school and go to college. It won't be easy. I believe in you baby. You have always been a strong young lady and resilient.

Don't forget you have people on your side
that can help you. You will also have
people that will tell you negative things.
God will give you the strength to keep
moving. Make sure you pray
continuously. He wants to hear from
you."

"Daddy, are you mad at me? Is God
mad at me?"

"No, I'm not mad at you neither is your
Heavenly Father. Ask Him to forgive you
for your sins. Remember how we used to
pray? You need to pray and talk to him.
You have to teach your son to pray. Make
sure you have men of God around him to
help you with him. They will help you
expose him to positive examples of men.
There will come a time when your boy
will need his father or at least a strong
male figure. You can't teach him to be a
man, only his dad can or another man.
Just like your mother can only teach you
how to be a young lady. I didn't know all
of the things a girl needed, your mother
did. It's the same with fathers and their
sons. Pray for a strong mentor to enter
his life. God will bring him to you.
You just have to ask and be aware
when he comes around."

Chapter Fourteen

LT take me by the Canyon. I need to go to my locker to get my backpack.

> "Man you ain't been to school in over
> a year. You don't have a locker no mo."

> "You ain't even knowin. I put some
> stuff in a locker for mergencies."

> "Okay. Les roll."

L.T. says and skids off. He only asks a few questions and is silent again. Upon arrival, to the school, I go straight to the old lockers that are near a storage area beside the gym. I'm hoping they didn't trash the lockers.

> "Look man, I'm not sure what you're
> up to, but what exactly went down
> the other night?"

L.T. needs some answers.

"Me and Omar did a drug deal. Some
fools rolled up on us and shot up the
car. Someone I never saw snatched
me out and left me on Big Mama's
street. Right in front of her house"

"A drug deal? Man, what's up witchu.
They could have killed you too."

"I know, but I was strapped. The only
problem is I don't know who they
are. I could be a sitting duck, so I
have to get out of the neighborhood
right now."

"What about Big Mama?"

"I can't worry about her. See, I told
you. It's still here"

I pull the backpack out of the locker. I open it, look inside, then
close it up.

"We good now. Lets go."

As we drive a few blocks from the school, I see that foo
Lawnboy.

"Pull over by this fool. I need to
talk to him."

I get out of the car.

"Aye foo! Hold up!"

Shawn stops.

"You talking to me?"

"Yeah Lawnboy!"

"What?"

"Where Jazmyn at? I know you know."

"I don't know."

"Why you been talking to my
cousin Mookie?"

"Who did you say? *Your cousin?*
Mookie?"

"Yeah foo! You heard me."

"Mookie and I are friends unlike
the fake cousin you claim to be."

"Friends! Friends! You ain't got no
friends and I got cho fake."

"Why you so concerned about me
and Mookie. You scared your lies
are gonna come out?"

I knock him off his bike. Before I know it, he is up and kicks
me across the face like a Ninja. He knows some kind of Karate
or something. I lay on the ground.

I taste blood, but before I get up Lawnboy pins me to the ground while sitting on top of me.

> "I know your secret and I'm telling
> Jazmyn."

Before anything else happens, L.T. comes over and pushes Lawnboy off me.

> "Man let's go before someone sees
> you. Don't waste your time on this kid."

We hop into the car and take off. There's silence for a span of at least five minutes. Then L.T. speaks.

> "Man, you were about to get
> your butt whooped."

> "Who! He wasn't gonna whoop
> me! Lil Punk!"

> "He had his arm in your throat and
> he KICKED you in your face."

I didn't say anything else about it. I'll take care of that little punk later. We pull up to the Four Seasons Hotel.

> "This you man? The Four Seasons?"

> "Yeah, you know nothin but the best
> for Malik."

I tell him.

"Alright stay safe; and stay away
from my house too."

"Bet! Thanks, dog for everything.
preciate chu.

Once I check in and get settled in my room. I feel instant
relief. I love a nice hotel bed.
After I get a good night sleep, I'll pay that little Lawnboy a
visit. Me and this gun will have a meeting with him first thing
in the morning.

Around midnight, I can hear the phone ringing from inside
my backpack. I'm glad the backpack was still in my locker
at school. Where am I? I'm a bit disoriented when I first open
my eyes. Then I realize I'm in the hotel. Thank goodness. The
only thing missing is my baby Jazz. I interrupt my thoughts to
read a text.

> *Mookie - Malik where you at?*
> *Big Mama is very*
> *upset. Where you at*
> *foo? I know you*
> *aint dead, answer me.*
> *Okay Foo don't answer*
> *me. Don't come anywhere*
> *near here or I will make*
> *sure you are the one that*
> *dies just like my cousin.*

How did he know? Oh! That foo Lawnboy said something. I
know it was him. I'll have to pay that fool a visit at his house in
the morning. I'll wait til his parents are not home or whoever
he lives with and smoke his lights out. I've seen where he lives

from back in the day when I was in school.

I'll smoke him like spareribs on a hot summer day. Ahh yes. Hurting him, before he goes off to tell Jazmyn, is a comforting thought that eases my mind while I fall asleep.

Hours into my rest I hear, Bam! Bam! Boom! There is a knock at the door that startles me. Is it the police? Whoever it is, they are knocking too hard. I get up and look through the peep hole.

It's housekeeping.

"What!" I yell through the door.

"Mr. Miller?"

"Yeah! What up?"

"Would you be needing your room cleaned today?"

I forgot to put the do not disturb sign out.

"No ma'am I'm fine. Thank you."

"Okay Mr. Miller. Let us know if you need anything else."

"Yeah, ok."

I walk away from the door to check the time. It's 9:00am! I gotta get outta here! On second thought, I think I'll shower first. I can't kill that fool smelling like this. It's been two days since I've been in some water. I get out the shower, get dressed, put my gun in my waistband, and take an Uber to his house. I quietly focus on what I'm about to do to this foo.

I do my best to appease this driver, who has yet to figure out that I'm not accustomed to holding a meaningless conversation. We finally arrive near Lawnboy's street. I have him drop me off at the corner.

I walk the rest of the way to his house. There are no cars in the driveway, so I assume no one is home except him. I creep down the driveway looking in the windows. I go into the backyard and check the sliding glass door. Bingo! It's unlocked! I'm in! I hear Lawnboy talking. It sounds like he's on the speaker phone talking to someone. I'll listen to his conversation.

> "Yeah man I'm gonna go up there
> to see Jazmyn, but she doesn't know
> I'm not the Sean she's been talking
> to. She thinks I'm some twenty-two
> years old with a Camaro. I spelled
> my name a little different thinking I
> can go undetected. She doesn't know
> Shawn at school."

> "Man, you lied to her? How do you
> think she's gonna feel when she
> sees you're the boy who works
> for her uncle or even worse the boy
> she shuns at school?"

I listen very closely. That voice Lawnboy is talking to sounds familiar. I'll listen some more.

> "Mookie Man, I started working for
> her uncle to be close to her. I love
> her, but I know she won't mess

with a guy like me. She's into Malik."

"Yeah, next time I see that foo I'm
gonna kill him."

"How, with a loaded backpack
and fruit snacks?"

"Don't worry about that, Imma
handle mine. I have what I need."

"How's Big Mama."

Lawnboy asks.

"She alright. Getting better. I think
she feels safe with those ex-FBI
agents hanging around the house."

"FBI?"

"Yeah, those two dudes in that
black Honda Accord."

"Oh yeah, they've been there for months."

"Malik's parents hired them to watch his
back. He mommy called Big Mama so
she wouldn't get suspicious with them
being in front of her house."

Mookie says sarcastically.

"Wow, I can't believe that dude.
He's as fake as an eighteen-dollar
bill. A real fake and a fraud!"

"A real fake and a fraud."

Enough, this is my cue to blast that room. I kick the door in.

"Lawnboy!"

He turns and looks at me. He's afraid but gets up. I have my gun pointed at his chest.

It's over for you homeboy!"

Lawnboy squeezes his eyes shut.

"Malik please put the gun down.
Don't kill me. We can talk about
whatever you want to talk about."

"I WANT TO KNOW WHERE
JAZMYN IS. YOU KNOW
WHERE SHE IS."

"I told you I don't know."

I fire the gun. It does nothing. It pops like a toy gun. Omar gave me a cap gun that looks real.

"What tha?"

I say looking at the gun in my hand. Before I can say anything else, Lawnboy jumps on me again. This time he used his fists and Karate. I fought back but I had to get out of there. When he let me up, I was able to see his airplane confirmation sitting on his desk. I pick up the stupid fake gun and run out the house.

"Malik! I can kill you. You have no idea
how lethal I am. You better run! You're
lucky that I don't chase you down, call
the cops and tell them you killed Omar.
I'm sure they are looking for you now!"

I just dash out the house the way I came in. I call another Uber
while running down the street. I meet the driver at a 7 Eleven
several blocks away. Ironically, it's the same verbose driver
who took me to Lawnboy's street. He knew exactly where to
take me. I just sit back and listen to him talk to himself all the
way to the hotel. Once I get to my room, I begin to make my
reservations for the first flight out early the next morning.
That stupid Lawnboy is leaving in the afternoon, that's much
too late to beat me. Hours before he shares his truth about
himself and me, I'll be at her aunt's house filling her head
with lies.

Chapter Fifteen

Baby Jay and I are settling into our routine pretty quickly. Especially since he's only days old. I seem to be getting used to the diaper changes, the early morning feedings, the early morning crying, the mid-day crying, the nightly crying and not sleeping too much. I feel so exhausted. While sitting on my bed my phone rings.

"Hi Uncle B!"

"Hey sweetie, how's my Baby Jay doing?"

"He's good."

"Oh, that's nice. I can't wait to see my nephew."

"Oh, I'm so excited. I can't wait to see you Uncle Benny. You're gonna fall in love with Jayson as soon as you see him. Do you know when you're coming?"

Baby Jay starts to squirm, but it isn't time to get up.

"Uncle Benny, let me call you back.
I need him to stay asleep. I love you."

"Okay Sweetie, I just wanted to check
on you. I'm proud of you. Let me know
if there's anything you need. I love you
too."

Baby Jay started to cry. He wanted to be held.

"I hear that baby. Go ahead and get
him. I'll talk to you later."

"Okay, bye."

Once I get the baby back to sleep, I call Sean. He doesn't
answer again. Why doesn't he answer my calls? It's just weird
how he acts so interested and when it comes to conversation
it's only through text. I don't like that.

Jazzy - Hey Sean what are you up to?
Sean - Hey Jazmyn, how are you?
Jazzy - Why is it that when I text you,
I get an answer right away.
If I call, there's no answer?
Sean - I'm at work.
Jazzy - Really?
Sean - Yes, why would I lie to you?
Jazzy - You tell me.
Sean - Come on baby. I wouldn't tell
you a lie. I'm working so, I
can't answer. I can always text
tho.
Jazzy - Well, do you still want to come

Let's see if he is still talking big stuff about coming to see me and the baby. He claims he misses me.

> *Sean – I'm going to try. I have a lot of*
> *work to do. You probably*
> *have to stay home and take*
> *care of the baby.*

Sean stopped texting abruptly. I'm so tired of these lying guys. I don't ever have to talk to any of them anymore. Malik is gone so I don't have to deal with him. I'm just gonna be single and stay that way. My son is my priority. I'm going to bed. Maybe tomorrow will be a better day.

Waaaaaaaa! Waaaaaa! Waaaaaaa! Baby Jay wakes me. I look at the clock. It's 7am. Feels like only ten minutes. Maybe it's because he woke me up a few times last night. Today, I want to just chill. Having a baby takes a lot out of you. Labor is just part of it. You have to cope with the pain and soreness that comes after it all. I'm still sore from having the baby. I've been told constantly to rest. So today that's what I'm going to do.

"Good morning my son."

I kiss my baby. He squirms and stretches. I wipe him down and get him ready for the day. I nurse him and put him down. I pick up my Bible and begin to read the book of Psalms to him. I can hear Auntie Noonie downstairs, praying and worshipping the Lord. I read a chapter and dress myself. Read another chapter, then dress the baby. I read another chapter, walk downstairs, so we can sit in the family room, and read some more. It takes much longer to get myself together since I can't move very fast. By the time I get downstairs, I hear the doorbell ring. Auntie is still praying when she answers the door.

"Hi, may I help you?"

"Yes, I'm here to see Jazmyn."

The person says. The voice sounds familiar. Is that Sean?

"Who are you?

"I'm her friend Sean."

Okay have a seat in the living room. I'll let her know you're here. OMG! Sean is here! He never said anything! I walk in the room holding Jay close. I'm confused. That's Lawnboy. That's not SexySean. He stands up.

"Hi Jazmyn."

"Hi, what are you doing here?"

"I need to talk to you."

"About what? We don't even know each other."

I decide I want to sit because I feel faint. Why did he come all the way out here? The only people who know that I'm here are family, Mimi, and *Sean?* No, this can't be Sean. I take a deep breath.

"Jazmyn, I came here because I need to be completely honest with you."

"Wait! What's your name?"

"Shawn."

"No, no, no, no." I shake my head.

"Jazmyn please listen to me. When I
met you online, I pretended to be
older. I did that because when I saw
you at school you never even looked
my way. I had to think of a way to
get you to talk to me."

I can feel tears welling up in my eyes. I'm holding them back.
Oh, I see Auntie. I see what this is. I think to myself. He tries
to speak, but I cut him off.

"Be quiet! No weapon formed
against me shall prosper in
the name of Jesus."

Baby Jay starts to cry. Auntie comes in to take him. Before she
leaves, she takes a long look at Shawn. There's a knock at the
door. Auntie walks over and looks through the peep hole.

"Who is it?"

"Mr. and Mrs. Miller."

She opens the door.

"Yes? May I help you?"

"Hi, we are here to see Jazmyn."

"Who are you?"

"May we come in?"

"Not until you tell me why you would like to see my niece."

"We're Michael's, I mean Malik's parents. We understand that our son has a baby. Is that our beautiful Grandchild in your arms?"

Auntie Noonie stops and looks back at me. She lets them in. I'm still sitting in my chair. I don't know who they are or what they want. They come in and walk over to me.

"Hi Jazmyn? I'm Cynthia Miller and this is my husband Dr. Chris Miller. We are Michael's parents. You know him as Malik."

"Oh wow. Ummm, hi."

I turn and glare at Shawn. He puts his head down.

"I really don't know where to start."

Auntie Noonie interrupts her.

"Try the beginning. That's where all stories start."

Mrs. Miller sighs.

"Well, Michael started running away from us about eight years ago."

Before she can continue, I interrupt her.

> "Mrs. Miller, I'm sorry to tell you
> this, but Malik or Michael was
> killed the day our baby was
> born."

I can feel the tears coming again. Shawn interrupts.

> "Jazmyn that's the other thing
> I wanted to tell you. Malik or
> Michael Miller, in this case,
> is not dead. He's alive."

> "How do you know all of this
> Shawn?"

He didn't answer.

> "Jazmyn, don't be hard on this
> young man. It's all Michael's
> fault."

Mrs. Miller says.

> "He's been doing this for years.
> He leaves us and wanders from
> city to city causing havoc
> wherever he decides to settle.
> This is the first time that he has
> gotten someone pregnant.
> We are really sorry, but we're
> going to put a stop to it now.
> That's why we're here. We're

here to take him home."

Auntie Noonie interrupts.

> "Home! Where exactly is that?
> He needs to provide a home
> for him."

She gestures while holding Baby Jay in her arms.

> "You're right, but first we have to
> get our hands on him. We know
> that he's coming to see Jazmyn.
> My associates and I are FBI
> agents. I've had them watching
> him for months to keep him safe."

Auntie Noonie cuts in.

> "So, you just let your son roam
> America like a flea bitten sex
> dog?"

> "My husband and I just want to
> make things right. We want to
> help with the baby in every
> way we can."

I remain silent.

> "How can you help? What do you
> want? Your son has caused so much
> damage to my niece. He even put
> hands on her."

"What! We didn't know that.

We are very sorry Jazmyn."

She pauses for what seems like hours, but it was only about
two minute.

> "For starters, we're offering help
> financially. I'm sure a bit of
> money for the baby will be helpful.
> Hopefully, we're a major part of his
> life as well. At least we'd like to be."

I can't be silent any longer.

> "Help me Jesus! For greater is He
> that is in me than he that is in
> the world. In the name of Jesus."

The doorbell rings. Auntie Noonie says,

> "There you go Jazz use the word
> to destroy the enemy."

Auntie Noonie gives me the baby back. He begins to cry.
Auntie Noonie walks over to the door to look out the peep
hole as Mrs. Miller says,

> "Awwww."

I leave the room to feed Baby Jay. I return to the room to sit
in a chair away from everyone to feel safe. I don't want to be
close to any of these people. I feel like they are out to wreck
my life. I don't pay any mind to anyone. I get myself
comfortable to focus on Baby Jay. I say to him,

"You don't want to hear these
crazy people. Let me rock
you to sleep."

A familiar voice shouts, "Jazmyn!" I freeze and say, "Malik?"
I look up and immediately start to cry. No more holding back.

He walks towards me. Then I say to Malik.

"STOP! Don't you dare come near me."

I stop crying. Suddenly, I feel stronger.

"Jazmyn, please can I talk to you?"

"Michael, come over here and
have a seat son."

Mr. Miller instructs him.

"This is too much."

I say, then Auntie Noonie speaks.

"Malik/Michael, whoever you
are. How dare you come to
my house unannounced after all
the pain you have caused my niece"

"Ma'am, Jazmyn won't answer
my calls. I didn't know what else
to do."

My emotions overtake me, and I speak.

"Why are you all here? I want you
all to leave. I want to go to bed
and end this nightmare. I want sleep."

"Ma'am do you think I can talk to
Jazmyn alone? I just need to talk
to her and explain some things. I
want her to forgive me for
anything and everything that I did
to her."

"Look here whoever you are. Talk
to her right there. She will not be
going into any rooms with you
alone."

"Jazmyn, I'm so sorry."

Shawn chimes in.

"You might want to start with
who you really are."

"Man, nobody is talking to you."

His mom is clearly agitated and speaks to Malik.

"Son, talk to her and ignore
all interruptions."

"Jazmyn my real name is Michael Miller.
I am a run-a-way. I was wandering the
streets one night and Big Moma had
compassion. She took me in.

I told her my situation, and she agreed to
let me live with her for however long I
wanted. I paid her rent monthly and she
kept my secret. In order to make it
believable, I had to pretend that Omar
was my brother. Everyone was down
with it. I thought it was all good since
my parents didn't come looking for
me this time. As long as Big Mama
got her money, she didn't care what I
did. That's why it was so easy to
drop out of school."

I start to cry again. I cannot get it under control.

"Malik. Michael. Why did you lie
to me? You said you loved me.
You lied."

"I'm sorry I lied about who I am,
but I didn't lie about loving you.
I have tried to text and call; but
you blocked me.

He pauses and looks at Baby Jay.

"Is this our son?"

I don't answer. I just look down at him. My precious baby in
all this chaos. I don't like it. I can't make any decisions.
Malik, or Michael's parents are here. Whoever he is today.
SexySean is here or whoever he is today. I have been living a
lie and didn't even know it.

"Jesus has given me the power to tread
on serpents and scorpions and all the
power of the enemy and nothing shall
by any means hurt me. Flee from me!
All of you in the name of Jesus."

Auntie Noonie begins to back me up.

"Okay you heard her, flee in the
name of Jesus. That's enough
information and apologies for
one day. You people have already
made it a long draining day and its
only noon. Jazmyn and I will
converse about relationships
with grandparents and the father
when she is good and ready. It's
her decision. Right now, it's time
to get out my house.

She holds the door for everyone to walk out. Malik turns to
me and says.

"Jazmyn please call or text me?"

I respond and say to him,

"Flee from me in the name of
Jesus. LEAVE! NOW!"

I look him in the eye. Malik's mom speaks.

"Jazmyn, I'll leave my card.
with you. You can call me
anytime. I will look forward
to hearing from you."

Auntie Noonie takes the card from her and speaks.

"It won't be guaranteed. Goodbye."

Sean looks at me and puts his head down. He didn't say
anything he just left. Malik is the last one to leave, but
he did leave. Auntie closes the door behind them. She
turns to me.

"Awww babygirl I'm so sorry."

I break down. She held me even sitting in the chair. She held
me so tight.

"You don't have to make any decisions until
you want to, but what I want you to do is
be strong. You have had a rough time in the
past few days. The good thing, you are a
child of God and he's got your back. There
is no need to cry all the time anymore.
This beautiful gift that you are holding is
enough to keep a smile on your face
forever."

"Auntie, Malik is supposed to be
dead. He's still alive."

I begin to cry.

"I know baby. It is a lot to digest, but
what kind of tears are those? Are those
tears of joy that he's alive or are you
feeling sorry for yourself because
he's alive and you really wanted him
dead? I'm going to leave you alone
to think about it. You can go lay down
or stay here. But just take some time
with your baby. Pray for strength. I
heard you put God's word on the
enemy. You got it. That's Who you
must trust in to truly make it. More
trials will come, but trust in the name
of Jesus. Also remember, we do not
wrestle against flesh and blood."

She leaves me there and I was happy to finally be alone. I
cried until I couldn't cry anymore. I cried again now for the
fact that Malik is alive. I don't know what that means for us,
but he's alive. I don't have to tell my son he doesn't have a
father. I need so many answers from him. I cried for the liar
that Shawn is and never want to see or hear his voice again.
And finally, I cried for the grandparents my son will have.
After I finished crying, I was curious about the things my aunt
said to me. I really have to ask her what is meant by "We do
not wrestle against flesh and blood." I stay in the living room
so long I start to doze off. I'm awakened by the doorbell again.
This time it startles me. Auntie Noonie answers the door. It
sounded like she was stomping to the door with angry feet.

"Who could this be now?"

She opened the door.

"Surprise!"

Uncle Benny and Auntie Rachel announce.

"Oh, my goodness! It is so good to
see you two. Jazmyn look who's here."

They walk in and both come eagerly to see me and the baby.

"Punkin, he's beautiful."

"Thank you Uncle Benny. He is."

"Yes, Jazmyn he is beautiful.
Congratulations."

Auntie Rachel says.

"Thank you, Auntie."

"Punkin your auntie's sole purpose
this week was on coming out here
to see this baby. She said we need
to help them right now, any way
we can. So here we are."

"Really?"

"Yes, Jazmyn. I've had time to
think about some things; and I owe
you a huge apology. I let some of
my own issues get in the way of a
real relationship that we could have
been building. I'm so sorry for the

way I have treated you.

God has worked on my heart. He let me
know that now is the time you really
need me. It's also the time I can be a
part of Jayson's life. I can help you
with anything you need. I have one
question for you."

I'm so stunned and speechless. Is this who I think it is?

"Auntie I don't know what to say.
What's your question?"

"Will you come back home?"

Another decision, but that's an easy answer. I have always
wanted a relationship with Auntie Rachel. Now is my chance
to bond with her. Her whole demeanor has changed. Auntie
Rachel is so much calmer. It's just weird. She doesn't seem
anything like she was. Can I trust her?

"Jazmyn, I have always loved you
and never knew how to express it.
Will you give me a chance?"

Uncle Benny interrupts.

"Punkin, we really want you to
come home and let us help you
with the baby."

"Okay, I really do want to come home. Auntie Noonie doesn't need me and a baby hanging around her house. I'll come home."

Auntie Noonie didn't dispute it because she knows where I need to be.

"Well, when you are able to travel, we will take you home. Benny will go back home in a few days, and I will stay here to help you out until we can leave. Is that okay with you sis?"

"That's a wonderful idea. I'm so happy that she will be home and her other auntie is finally willing to help."

I begin to talk to my baby.

"You hear that Jayson? We are going home. Lord, I give you the glory, the honor and the praise. Thank you in the name of Jesus."